Her Place in Time

Other Books by Stephenia H. McGee

Ironwood Plantation
The Whistle Walk
Heir of Hope
Missing Mercy
*Ironwood Series Set
*Get the entire series at a discounted price

The Accidental Spy Series
*Previously published as The Liberator Series

An Accidental Spy
A Dangerous Performance
A Daring Pursuit
*Accidental Spy Series Set
*Get the entire series at a discounted price

Stand Alone Titles
In His Eyes
Eternity Between Us

Time Travel
Her Place in Time
(Stand alone, but ties to Rosswood from The Accidental Spy Series)
The Hope of Christmas Past
(Stand alone, but ties to Belmont from In His Eyes)

Novellas
The Heart of Home
The Hope of Christmas Past

www.StepheniaMcGee.com
Sign up for my newsletter to be the first to see new cover reveals and be notified of release dates
New newsletter subscribers receive a free book!
Get yours here
bookhip.com/QCZVKZ

Her Place in Time

STEPHENIA H. MCGEE

Dear reader,

When I first visited the Rosswood Plantation while researching for The Accidental Spy Series, I made an interesting discovery. Miss Jean, the wonderful lady that owns the house (and mother of Mr. Ray Hylander, who you will have the pleasure of meeting in the story) told me how they found a yellow Civil War era gown in a trunk in the attic. They believe it may have belonged to Mabella, Rosswood's historical lady.

Miss Jean allowed me to see the dress, gently clip to my shoulders, and take a few pictures with it. While posing with the gown, I had a wild idea. What if by putting it on, someone could travel back in time? Thus, the story was born. And, dear reader, that is all it is meant to be.

This story is not meant to spark a theological debate on if God would allow the miracle of time travel. Second Corinthians tells us that when we are away from our earthly bodies, Christians go to the presence of the Lord. Hebrews 9 teaches it is appointed to men once to die. Knowing these things, I do not mean to say I believe in any kind of reincarnation by allowing my character to have a life in two different eras.

Several of the things regarding the time-slip in the story are not possible, but it allows us to suspend what we know to be true to simply enjoy the fictional freedom of the *what if…?* So, come with me, imaginative reader. Let's go discover a mysterious gown and see what it might be like to step back in time…

Happy Reading!
Stephenia

Chapter One

Lorman, Mississippi
Late October, Present Day

If only leaving her problems behind were as simple as leaving town. Lena drummed her fingers on the faded paint on the car door and watched the landscape slide by. Wind spilled through the open window, teasing strands of her hair free and whipping them around her face. She thought to brush them away but decided against it. She might as well enjoy the feeling while she still had the chance.

"Are you even listening to me, Amberlena Elizabeth?"

Lena blinked and turned her attention from the passing trees to her mother's concerned expression. Any time Momma used Lena's full name, she meant business. "Sorry, Momma. I was just thinking."

Momma reached across the narrow console in her vintage Volkswagen bug and squeezed Lena's hand. "We promised we wouldn't think on that for two whole days." Tears filled Momma's deep brown eyes, but she shooed them away with an overstuffed smile.

Lena fashioned a smile of her own, though her lips seemed to strain against the falsity. She'd promised they would enjoy this mother-daughter trip and pretend life wouldn't be waiting for them when they got home. And Momma certainly deserved the break. If it would make her happy, then Lena would gladly pretend. She brightened her tone. "Tell me something about this one."

Momma wiped away the lingering drops of reality from her eyes and cut on the blinker. "They say some of the guests have seen a man and woman walking arm in arm on the front lawn." Her voice held a mixture of humor and awe. Momma always did like a good ghost story, even if she didn't technically believe in them.

Lena leaned forward and studied the big white house looming at the end of the long drive. Four massive white columns supported the two-story mansion, another testament to what Momma called *the age when cotton was king*. Deciding to tease Momma a little, she shrugged. "What's so special about that? No couples allowed on the lawn?"

Momma rolled her eyes. "You hush now. You know what I mean. They say he's still in his Confederate uniform and she's wearing one of those big hoop dresses."

"They probably paid actors to cause a stir."

Momma grinned. "Guess we'll find out." She pulled up to the side of the house and parked underneath an ancient oak. After giving Lena a wink, she hopped out.

Lena paused with her hand on the door handle and drew three deep breaths. Two days to spend with Momma and try to forget. Two days out in the fresh country air with nothing to do but chat and remember the good times. To have one last retreat before...

"Come on now, Lena," Momma said, poking her head back inside the car. "What are you waiting on?"

Lena swung the door open, placed one worn tennis shoe onto vibrant grass, and stepped from the car. Birds trilled and flitted around in the branches overhead, the stately tree having not yet decided to don its golden autumn gown. Lena flung her bag over one shoulder and rounded the front of the car to help Momma get the latch unstuck. Volkswagens were strange like that, with the trunk in the front and the engine in the back. Part of the charm, Momma always said.

"You know, you really need to get something a bit more reliable," Lena said, pushing on the trunk. "I had my doubts this thing would even get us down here."

Momma wrenched the handle and the trunk popped free. "Nonsense. Betty here is an old friend."

Lena didn't bother replying. What would have been the point? She reached in and grabbed Momma's overnight bag, its fraying edges a testament to Momma's motto of *use it up, wear it out, make it last, or do without.* As a single mother with more determination than formal education, Momma had her reasons for how she saw life. Degree or not, she was still the smartest person Lena knew.

Momma took the bag with a smile a bit too cheery.

"Ready?"

A lump in Lena's throat kept her from answering. Would this really be their last trip together? She swallowed the thought and wrapped her arm around Momma's shoulders. They climbed the front steps to the massive house and stood on the porch. Lena looked up at the blue porch ceiling while Momma knocked on the door.

Momma had always loved these old houses. She reveled in the history, the stories, and the grandeur of the antebellum age. She'd almost named Lena *Bonnie Blue* after Scarlett's daughter in *Gone with the Wind*, but thankfully had changed her mind. Though Amberlena Elizabeth was bad enough.

The front door swung open, and they were greeted by a tall, stately looking gentleman with a friendly face and graying hair. "You must be the Lowrey ladies down from Jackson. I'm Ray Hylander." He pulled the door wider. "Welcome to Rosswood."

Momma bustled in, her big brown eyes flitting over everything in the entry. Lena smiled at the gentleman. "Nice house."

Momma waved a hand. "Manners, darling." She turned and looked up at the tall man. "I'm Celia Ann, and this is my daughter, Lena Beth."

Lena stuck out her hand. "Just Lena is fine."

Momma made a face, but Lena ignored it. Mr. Hylander shook her hand and then fished a key from his pocket. "I have your room ready, ladies, if you would like to put your things down." He turned and started up a staircase at the end of the long, wide entryway and

Lena and Momma followed. At the top of the stairs another wide hallway boasted a seating area and cases filled with books, the hallway itself a kind of open-ended living room. It looked like a perfect place to sit and read.

Their host turned the key and opened the door to one of the rooms, revealing period furniture and high ceilings. Exactly the kind of place Momma swooned over. Lena smiled to herself. This had been a good choice. It would make Momma happy, and she'd need some of that happiness to carry into the days to come.

"Peggy serves breakfast at nine," Mr. Hylander said, calling them back from Momma's twittering over the room. "You won't want to miss that. Finest homemade biscuits in the South."

Momma shot Lena a grin. "Our mouths are watering already."

"We also have a library downstairs you're welcome to use," he said, "and there are some journals left from the plantation days."

Momma clasped her hands. "Oh! How exciting."

Mr. Hylander's lips turned up. "Soon as you get settled, I'd be happy to give you ladies the tour and tell you about the history of the house."

"Thank you, sir. We're looking forward to it." Momma took the key from him, promising they would be down in a bit, and shut the door. She patted the curly hair she'd passed down to Lena. "Isn't this great?"

Lena's lips curved. "You'll have to bring Carl down here sometime."

Momma's eyes widened. "Lena! What a thing to

say. Bringing a man to a bed-and-breakfast." She scrunched her nose. "That would be quite an inappropriate invitation."

"Why? You can get two rooms."

Momma rolled her eyes.

"Or a wedding band…"

Momma blushed and waved her hand. "Oh, you hush now."

Lena grew serious. "He's a good man, Momma, and I know you like him. A lot. Why do you always hold back?" Momma frowned, but Lena held up a hand to stay the words she knew Momma would say next. "Things are different now. You no longer have a child to care for on your own."

She stepped closer and put her hands on Momma's shoulders. "You're only thirty-nine. You need to let yourself have a life. You've spent every moment since you were seventeen taking care of me. And now…" She cleared her throat. "Momma, I don't want you to be alone."

Momma's eyes glistened. "We aren't talking about that, remember?"

Lena pulled her closer. "We don't have to talk about it now, but you still need to think on it. It's time you found some happiness, and I think Carl would go a long way to helping you find it."

Momma waved her hand again, shooing away anything she didn't want to discuss. "I'm going downstairs to ask our host about recommendations for where to eat supper tonight." She pointed a finger at Lena. "And when I come back up here, you are going to be ready for our tour, right?"

"Yes, ma'am."

Momma smiled. "Good girl. I'll be right back."

Lena's shoulders slumped as soon as Momma closed the door. She shouldn't keep pushing. Momma deserved exactly what she'd asked for—one weekend without all the concerns that plagued them back home.

She turned to a large wardrobe on the wall. She'd unpack their clothes while she waited. She averted her gaze from the reflection taunting her from the inset mirror and pulled open the carved wardrobe door. Inside, a yellow gown with yards of ruffled fabric took up one end. Odd. She pulled it out.

It looked old but in good condition. The gauzy material draped across the neckline, and the skirt was made of layers of delicate ruffles. Lena laughed. She'd been right. This must be one of the costumes they had the actors wear to walk around and make guests think Civil War couples still roamed the grounds!

She held it up to her and shut the wardrobe door. The mirror there showed her the reflection she'd avoided looking at for weeks now. She ignored the sallow cast to her skin and the dullness of her muddy brown hair and focused on the dress. It looked like it would fit.

Did she dare? It might upset the owner if he saw her in the costume someone had forgotten to hide from the guests, but Momma would be thrilled. And that would be worth it. Before she could change her mind, Lena slipped out of her jeans and blouse and tugged the gown over her head, fastening the hooks behind her neck.

A wave of nausea overcame her, and she closed her eyes, gripping the bedpost. They were getting more frequent now. Lena pulled long breaths into her lungs and let them out slowly until the sensation passed and the room stopped spinning. Then she straightened and ran her fingers over the material.

Huh. It seemed a much brighter yellow on her than it had when it was hanging in the wardrobe. The ruffles fell all the way to the ground.

Lena propped her hands on her waist. The dress fit almost as if it had been made for her. She giggled, feeling much better. Momma would get a kick out of this for sure. She kept her eyes away from the mirror and tugged her curls into a bun at the nape of her neck. Now. Surely she looked the part.

Footsteps sounded in the hall, and Lena turned toward the door. Wouldn't Momma be surprised? The doorknob turned, and Lena gripped the sides of her skirt, pulling it up so she could curtsy when Momma came inside.

But when the door swung open, it wasn't Momma standing stunned in the hallway. A woman who looked a little younger than Lena saw her and stumbled back, her blue eyes wide in shock. Lena yelped and dropped the skirt. Heat crawled into her face as the actress, who wore an even more authentic dress than the one Lena had found, gaped at her. Lena gulped.

Busted.

The woman grabbed the cotton fabric at the base of her throat and then her eyes narrowed. "Who are you? What are you doing here?"

"I, uh, this is the room that Mr. Hylander gave us."

Her face contorted. "Who?"

"Mr. Hylander," she repeated, speaking slowly. "You know, the fellow who owns this bed-and-breakfast? This is the room he gave us." She stepped back. "I'm sorry about the dress. Give me a second to change and then we can go downstairs. I'm sure he can clear this up. I didn't realize he'd mistakenly given us an actor's room." She winked at the gaping woman. "But don't worry, I'll pretend I didn't see you. You can still do your thing for Momma. She'll like it."

The woman stared at her. "Miss, I don't know who you are or what kind of farce you are trying to conduct here, but this is *my* house." She frowned. "And we *don't* take any painted ladies for the soldiers. Best you be moving on."

"What?" Painted ladies? This woman...no, girl, really, took her part far too seriously. "This is a bed-and-breakfast. Momma and I are staying..." Her words died as the blonde girl adamantly shook her head.

"Rosswood belongs to me. You'll have to look for your man elsewhere."

Man? Now what nonsense was she talking about? Annoyed, Lena pursed her lips and stepped around her, meaning to go downstairs and have a word with the owner about his actors taking their roles entirely too far. But when she stepped into the hall, the sight before her nearly buckled her knees. Suddenly, a stench that could have curdled the wallpaper rushed over her, making her stomach heave. How had she not noticed it before? She wrapped an arm around her middle, begging her body to behave as the scene unfolded.

This couldn't be happening. Not yet. Not now.

"Miss, you need to go." The girl's agitated voice *seemed* real.

But then, so did those men, and... *No!*

No. She couldn't start hallucinating yet. The doctor had said she had more time...

Lena began to pant, the sickening smells of un-washed bodies and blood taking hold of her olfactory senses and making her body believe they were real. Nausea washed over her again, and her vision began to fade.

A man's voice called out, but Lena slipped to the floor, her mind's cruel trick fading into oblivion. Darkness enveloped her, reminding her of all the things she was supposed to be forgetting this weekend, and swept her away to a land of cold indifference.

Chapter Two

What he wouldn't give for some release from this monotony. Something to distract him from the long wait to return to duty…and the humiliation of his missing eye.

Sergeant Caleb Dockery focused on the men around him, at least the best he could in his condition, and wondered if they felt the same. Private Paul Jenkins looked at Caleb over his cards, offering a smile that came often and easy to his thin lips. Now there was a man who seemed to have no trouble finding contentment in whatever condition he found himself. Even his long bout with pneumonia didn't seem to dampen his spirits.

Sergeant Wells looked at Caleb as well, appearing impatient. Was it his turn? He couldn't remember. His mind had wandered again. Then the sergeant swiveled, the rising voices on the other side of the upper hall in this makeshift hospital drawing the eyes of every pitiful soul forced to tarry here.

They all watched as a young woman bounded into

their midst and then collapsed in a heap of sunflower frills. She looked like a wilted flower, her delicate sensibilities too fragile for the realities of war. A shame, that. They'd worked too hard to protect their women from the more unpleasant things in life only for them to be doused by the worst of humanity now.

Miss Ross, the poor young woman whose unfortunate honor it had been to open her house up as a hospital, put her hands on her hips. "Peggy!"

Caleb shifted and tried to get a better look through his good eye. The colored woman who always hovered by Miss Ross's side shuffled over, her hands filled with the strips of cloth they'd been using for bandages.

"Lawd, what be goin' on here?"

Miss Ross scowled. "I don't know. Seems this lady is a bit confused about where she is. She worked herself into a dither and then had a spell."

Peggy knelt and put a hand on the lady's shoulder. Caleb leaned to the side to get a better look at the woman who had succumbed to the flutters. What was she doing wearing such a thing in a hospital? And in late afternoon, no less?

"You got any smellin' salts?" Peggy asked.

"You know I don't." Miss Ross glanced around at the staring men and lowered her voice, though Caleb had no trouble hearing her anyway. "Why would you even ask?"

The other woman huffed. "Never know what you be up to. You is liable to get your hands on all kinds of stuff. 'Member that chloroform?"

Miss Ross's blue eyes widened. "Hush! You know

good and well that was your fault, too."

Caleb couldn't help but chuckle at the absurdity of the scene. He'd grown accustomed to the banter between these two who acted more like friends than slave and mistress, but the fact that they chose to jab one another while one of their nurse maids laid unresponsive on the floor struck him as out of sorts. Both women's eyes darted to him.

Caleb cleared his throat. "Beg your pardon, Miss Ross, but what are you going to do about the lady on the floor?"

"Oh!" Miss Ross reached down and tugged on the woman's arm, giving her a good shake. "Miss? Miss you need to wake up."

The woman in yellow stirred, her eyes fluttering open and then widening in horror. She scrambled to her feet, tripping over her dress and would have landed on the floor again, if not for the maid, who gripped her arm firmly to steady her.

"What on earth is going on here?" The lady looked around the hall, her gaze traveling across the room and growing ever more horrified as she took in Caleb, then the other men at cards, and finally the three other fellows bedded down. "Why are these people here?"

"Wounded men that needs tending," Peggy said, eyeing the woman as though she were mad. From the looks of her, Caleb made the same assessment.

The woman squeezed her eyes shut. "This isn't happening. I was supposed to have more time."

When she opened her eyes again a few heartbeats later, disappointment clouded their almond-colored depths. Well, not that he could blame her. He was disappointed he was here as well. But she had a choice. He didn't.

She blinked at him as though she didn't believe what she saw. They stared at one another, even though Caleb knew he should avert his gaze from her humiliation. But the helplessness in her gaze stirred him, urging him to do something to alleviate her distress. Or perhaps he merely welcomed the break in the endless monotony.

Miss Ross took the woman's elbow and turned her toward the stairs. "Come on now, miss…"

"I'm Lena."

"Lena…?"

"Lena Lowrey."

"Oh?" Miss Ross said in a soothing way. "Any relation to the general?"

Miss Lowrey blinked at her. "What general?"

Peggy tucked the bandages under her arm and moved to the woman's other side, her voice taking on the gentle tone one uses with people who don't possess all of their wits. "Why, General Lowrey of course, child. The one they call the Preacher General. You be any relation to him?"

"I, um, distantly, I think but…"

Miss Ross exchanged a look with Peggy. "Come on now, dear. Best we get you on home."

The woman wrenched her arm away and took a step back. She put her fingers on her temples. "So much worse than I thought."

Caleb rose. Poor girl. She wasn't fit for a place like

this. "Miss Ross, I don't think this lady will be much help to you. She's too delicate of a flower."

The woman's eyes flew wide, and then she pinned him with a glare. "Now, you listen here, Mr. Reenactment Man. You people take this crazy stuff way too far. Scaring the tourists just to get a few extra dollars. The nerve!" She took a step toward him, and he quickly realized his initial assessment of her had been entirely incorrect. She pointed a finger at him in the most unladylike fashion. "I came here to have a relaxing weekend with my mother, not get bombarded by a bunch of ridiculous low-budget actors who can't seem to remember the stupid war ended over a hundred and fifty years ago!"

Caleb's mouth fell open.

Peggy grabbed Miss Ross. "She plumb mad, Miss Belle! We better get her to the doctor man right quick."

Miss Ross drew her eyebrows low and studied the terrified woman by her side. "Yes. I should have known when she turned up in my bedroom wearing an evening gown that she was a—" she lowered her voice—"A witless woman."

"I am *not* witless! What's the matter with you people?" Miss Lowrey snatched her long skirts and hiked them nearly to her knees, revealing completely bare, smooth calves and small feet ensconced in tiny white stockings that didn't even cover her ankles. He turned his head, mortified for her.

Miss Ross squealed. "Cover yourself! I'll have no indecent women in my house, witless or not!"

"That's it! You should be fired!"

Caleb couldn't help it. He reached out to help just in time to see the mad woman flee down the stairs.

"Momma!" Lena bounded down the stairs, her pulse pounding furiously. "Momma! Where are you?"

Even downstairs in the massive front hall, the hallucination relentlessly assaulted her in the form of groaning men scattered across the floor. She'd never been into history like her mother. So then, why had her mind chosen *this* of all things to assault her with? No. It wasn't a hallucination. It couldn't be.

These people were entirely too *real*. They had to be actors. Very fast actors who could set up very quickly…for an audience of two people.

In the foyer, a man in a gray uniform lay on a wooden cot in the main hallway, half of his leg missing. The stump was covered in a bloody bandage. In the other room, someone screamed. The man with the bloody stump grabbed her hand.

"Water, please," he groaned. His fetid breath washed over her.

She pulled her hand free and stumbled away. "Momma!"

The African-American woman from upstairs grabbed her elbow. "Steady there, miss. Now how 'bout you tell us where you come from?"

Lena blinked, trying to calm herself. "I came from Jackson with my mother. We checked in with Mr.

Hylander." Her throat constricted. "Peggy was supposed to make breakfast at nine."

The older woman's eyes widened. "Who done told you I'd make you breakfast?"

Uh-oh. "Are you Peggy?"

The blonde girl stepped up to them, eyeing Lena cautiously. "She is."

Well, that explained it. She'd dreamed the entire thing. Getting here with Momma, the man at the door, and the lady making breakfast. Her mind had conjured up this grisly Civil War scene because, secretly, she really hadn't wanted to go to an old plantation. Lena let out a deep breath. She closed her eyes.

She'd wake up any time now.

When she opened them, nothing had changed. Fine. Might as well let it play out. She never remembered realizing she was dreaming while still asleep before. It seemed rather surreal.

A man in a crisp uniform strode up to them, casting the man with a stump an assessing glance. "Has anyone seen to this soldier?" His cold gaze swept down Lena. "Who's this?"

"That's what we be tryin' to figure out."

The soldier ignored Peggy and spoke to the younger woman instead. "See that you do." He narrowed his eyes at Lena. "And see that she is properly dressed for work or that she's out of my way."

Lena ground her teeth. This dream only got more annoying. She grabbed the ruffled skirts and tromped toward the front door. Maybe if she could get out of the house, she could escape this nightmare.

She flung open the door, ignoring the comments of the figments of her damaged mind, and stepped out into the sunlight.

Chapter Three

$\mathcal{C}$ elia Ann thanked their host for the information and promised to come straight back as soon as she fetched her daughter. She took the stairs slowly, letting her hand trail along the smooth railing.

Lord, if there is any other way...

She left the prayer unfinished, knowing her Heavenly Father already understood Celia's heartache. It seemed unfair to lose Lena this soon. Her baby had just turned twenty-three. She should be on the brink of starting her life, not losing it. Celia topped the stairs, making her way past period furniture. The large door at the end of the hall stood ajar. Had Lena gone out to the balcony for a bit of air? To her knowledge, no other guests were currently staying with them.

Celia opened the door and slipped out onto the grand second-story porch. Fine molding topped the massive white pillars, and the space was decorated with wicker patio furniture. This would be a great place for the two of them to sit and talk.

But Lena wasn't up here. She turned to go back

inside.

"Momma!"

"Lena?"

Lena's voice seemed far away. Celia turned around and stepped up to the balcony railing, her fingers clutching the white paint. The land spread out in front of her, green fields that had long ago held cotton, and then a Christmas tree farm in later years. Celia scanned the yard, wondering if Lena had gone to the car looking for her. A girl in a bright yellow dress ran down the front steps of the house, ruffles streaming behind her down the brick walk.

Celia gripped the railing. Surely Lena hadn't been playing dress up.

The girl hurried past the angel statue surrounded by roses, heading toward the little iron gate set in the low wall at the front of the lawn. Then she seemed to blur, and Celia rubbed her eyes. She must be more exhausted than she thought.

When she lowered her hand, the girl had disappeared.

Lena groaned, the throbbing in her head pulsating through her eyes. She rolled to her back, realizing she was on the hard floor.

"Lena!"

She put her arm over her eyes to shield herself from the light. "Momma?"

"Oh, darling." Momma dropped to the floor beside her and put Lena's head in her lap. "What happened?"

Lena blinked, letting her eyes adjust to the light. Momma's worried face settled into focus. "I'm...not sure."

"Did you get dizzy again?"

She sucked air through her nose, and thankfully, no scents of blood and death clung to it. What a terrible nightmare! "Yes. I was going to surprise you, but I got nauseous, and then..." She shrugged. Better not tell Momma about the strange hallucination. It would only make her worry more.

"There now, you're all right now. Is the pain fading?"

She nodded. Back to the mild discomfort of constant pressure behind her forehead. Funny how she hadn't noticed it in her dream world. She'd felt stronger there, too. Her damaged brain was probably trying to compensate.

Momma pulled her to her feet, and Lena steadied herself.

"Do you need to rest? I can tell Mr. Hylander we will do the tour later."

"No," Lena said, brushing at her jeans. "I'm..." Wait. What happened to the yellow dress? She was sure she'd put that on *before* the incident. Or had that been part of the dream too?

Momma waited, then gently prompted, "You're what?"

Lena straightened her blue blouse, glancing at the wardrobe on the wall. If she opened it, would she find a yellow dress inside? "I'm feeling much better now. I'm sorry I frightened you."

Momma wrapped an arm around her shoulders. "No need to apologize."

They made their way down the stairs, Momma keeping a tight grip on Lena's hand the entire way. They found Mr. Hylander standing in the foyer at a round table situated under a sparkling chandelier. He offered them a pamphlet and then directed them to one of the front rooms.

"This is the library," he said, indicating a massive shelving unit against the back wall. "We have pages from the original owner's diary, which you are welcome to read." He gestured toward a carved desk against the wall, which contained laminated pages. "We plan on doing a little remodeling after the fall pilgrimage season. I aim to tear out these shelves and put in a new set."

"Oh," Momma said. "Will that cause any damage?"

"They are beginning to sag, I'm afraid. We want to have them repaired prior to the Christmas season."

They followed along as the host took them through the house, giving the history and pointing out interest-ing items. Under the staircase, a door led them to the basement, where slaves and household servants once lived. The space consisted of brick walls, two fireplaces, and some hand-carved beds with ropes that would have supported the mattresses. Momma seemed fascinated with it all, and Lena withheld her yawns as best she could.

Finally Mr. Hylander led them back to the main floor, continuing to give a history of the house. "... and for a time, Rosswood served as a hospital."

The words snagged her attention. "Did you say hospital?"

Momma smiled at her, apparently pleased she'd been paying attention.

"The lady of the house tended the sick, and many of the soldiers were buried out on the grounds." Mr. Hylander turned off the light to the basement area and closed the door.

Lena's pulse quickened. She hadn't known anything about a hospital. Why, then, had her mind conjured it? A shiver ran down her spine. "Can you tell me about the lady you said helped them?"

"During that time, a young woman by the name of Annabelle Ross lived here. She was the one old family lore says tried to help stop the Lincoln assassination."

Lena put her hand on the wall to steady herself. What was happening to her?

Momma's arm instantly went around Lena's waist. "Mr. Hylander, I think my daughter needs a nap. Can we please finish the tour later?"

"Certainly." He indicated the door at the back of the wide hall, beyond the staircase. "I'll be just through there if you need anything."

Momma thanked him and guided Lena back up the staircase. She wanted to argue against the nap. It would steal the time they wanted to spend together, but with the way her head was acting, maybe she needed it.

She let Momma fuss over her and tuck her into one of the two canopied beds in their room and then closed her eyes as Momma quietly left. Lena tugged the covers

under her chin, praying the pain in her head would ease
and her mind would clear. Then she drifted to sleep.

Miss Ross's screech made Caleb drop his cards. Sergeant
Wells, his partner in this round of euchre, scolded him.

"Hey now, you're showing your hand!"

Caleb slapped his hand over the cards, rattling the
table between them. He smoothly scooped the cards up
and turned them over.

Paul Jenkins followed Caleb's gaze and voiced the
question even as it formed in Caleb's mind. "Wonder
what the lady is having a conniption over?"

Sergeant Wells harrumphed. "What's it matter?"
He gestured toward Caleb. "It's your turn."

"I'll take my turn in a moment." Caleb excused
himself and stood, wondering what could be happening
now. Miss Ross and her maid had returned upstairs after
the strange woman departed, but had barely closed the
door to the chamber across from him before causing a
stir once more.

He rapped his knuckles on the door, ignoring the
grumbles of his fellows. "Miss Ross? Is something the
matter?"

The door flung open, and Miss Ross stared at him
with wide eyes. "We are fine, thank you."

"But I heard…" He lifted himself on his toes to
look over her head. The mad woman from earlier this
morning sat in the bed, rumpled covers around her

waist. She seemed confused. He looked away, embarrassed to have witnessed a lady in a compromised position.

It would seem Miss Lowrey had not vacated the premises after all. But when had she returned above stairs? None of them had noticed her. Caleb looked at Miss Ross and lowered his voice. "Shall I escort the lady home?"

Miss Ross glanced over her shoulder. "That would be well and good, except that she hails from a town near Jackson. She claims to have arrived at Rosswood with her mother, though I've seen no sign of the other lady." She leaned closer, speaking in a whisper. "Miss Lowrey also insists they arrived this morning in Volk's wagon." Miss Ross wagged her head. "But I have no knowledge of a Mr. Volk and do not understand why he would leave her at Rosswood."

Caleb considered a moment. "What are you going to do with her, then?"

"A pertinent question, sir, but one I am afraid I don't have an answer for. I came to my room and found her in my bed. I thought she'd left."

The young lady in question scrambled off the mattress in a wave of bedclothes and fabric. "Not *again!*"

Miss Ross let out a weary sigh.

"You go about your duties, ma'am. I'll try to get the lady calm and see if she can remember anything more."

Miss Ross hesitated a moment, then nodded. "See that she doesn't get into any trouble, will you, Sergeant?"

He inclined his head as Miss Ross passed by and admonished Sergeant Ackerman for being out of bed to play cards. Caleb withheld his smile, knowing the poor fellow needed something to take his mind off his missing foot. Any man would gladly shoulder Miss Ross's scolding for a few moments of distraction from something of that caliber.

The lady in the bedchamber seemed to have righted herself, and Caleb let his gaze travel to the confused young woman once more. When had she come back up here? He'd seen her flee below about an hour ago. Perhaps he'd been too involved in his game to notice her return.

She had a spray of glistening brown curls, which she'd pulled into a simple knot at the back of her head, and wide brown eyes set in a face that looked as though it was no stranger to the sun. A working woman in a lady's gown? She clasped slender fingers in front of her and seemed rather annoyed with his scrutiny. He stared anyway, unable to bring proper manners to bear.

"You." She pointed at him. "What day is it?"

He scratched the bandage around his head. "September the ninth, I believe." He shrugged. "But I haven't been too diligent in keeping count."

"Year?"

Poor woman truly was mad. "Still eighteen sixty-four, ma'am."

She tilted her head back and looked up at the ceiling. "Why now? Why not a dream when the country *isn't* in the middle of a war?"

Caleb watched her, feeling sorry for her confusion.

"Miss, is there someone nearby who might be looking for you?"

She turned her flashing gaze on him again. "It's only a dream. Why would anyone be looking for me?"

He crossed into the room and offered his arm, but she stepped away from him, wary. He tried for a gentle tone, one he hadn't had much use for in the army. "I mean only to offer you my assistance, and perhaps show you that I am real and not of a dream."

She stared at him for a moment, then placed her hand upon his proffered forearm. Strangely, her nails were dyed a warm pink. He withheld comment. When he didn't disappear under her touch, she seemed disappointed.

"Well, of course I would dream you solid."

"I can assure you, this is not a dream." He offered a friendly smile. "Do you remember how you got here? Perhaps I can locate Mr. Volk for you."

"Who?"

Worse than he thought. Seems she didn't remember what she'd told Miss Ross. How could he know if anything she said was real or imagined? He repeated the other part of the question. "Do you remember why you came to Rosswood?"

She huffed and stepped away from him. "Of course I do! I'm not crazy."

Her forehead crinkled, creating little lines along her brow. He tried to guess her age. A score of years, perhaps? He waited patiently until she relented.

"Fine. Momma wanted a girl's weekend." She moved her hands around as she spoke, animated. "We drove down from Jackson to stay at the Rosswood bed-and-breakfast. But every time I close my eyes, I end up dreaming these crazy vivid dreams about Civil War soldiers!"

"Hmm." Girl's weekend? What did that even mean? Would not this lady and her mother both be women? And what, pray tell, was a *bed-and-breakfast?* Did she refer to an inn? He brightened. "Oh! You have been misinformed, Miss Lowrey. Rosswood serves as a hospital, not an inn."

She gave him a flat stare. "Sure. Back in the Civil War. Now it's a bed-and-breakfast."

"Do you refer to the War of Northern Aggression?"

She laughed, though he did not find such a thing humorous.

"Yes. Southerners called it that, I guess, or the War Between the States and the Northerners called it the War of the Rebellion. Now we just call it the *Civil War.*" She lifted slim shoulders. "Ha! Wouldn't Momma be happy I know all that."

Caleb rubbed the back of his neck, trying to make sense of the words that poured out of her.

She straightened, revealing the curve of a graceful neck. "In any event, the war lasted from eighteen sixty-one to eighteen sixty-five, then ended just before Lincoln was assassinated."

"What?"

She narrowed her eyes. "But of course, Mr. Reenactor Man, you already know all of that. Please, just drop the character."

He had to remind himself to keep his mouth closed, lest it come unhinged. He stepped closer and took her arm, lowering his voice. "Miss, I don't know who you are or what you are doing here, but you best keep your ravings quiet."

Her eyes widened, but then she shook her head. "This is just a dream. What difference would that make?" She tilted her head. "Though it is a strikingly vivid one." Sadness crept into her features. "I suppose it's because of my condition."

Ah. So she was aware she was mad? "Condition?"

"I have stage four glioblastoma in my frontal lobe. Hard to operate on, but…"—she straightened with what appeared to be practiced resolve—"we are going to try."

How could the woman seem so lucid while spouting nonsense?

She crossed her arms. "I get that look a lot. It means I have a brain tumor." She put her finger on the center of her forehead. "Right here."

"Oh!" He suddenly felt ashamed. He'd once seen one of the men in his unit develop a tumor in his stomach. The bulging mass had eventually caused the soldier's death. Despite his better sense of manners, he peered closer at her. She seemed healthy. Well, aside from her lack of senses.

"You can't see it." She rolled her eyes toward the ceiling.

"Then how do they know it's there?" His fingers itched to pluck at the bandage over his lost eye, but he kept his hands firmly at his sides.

She picked at a thread on her gown. "You know, CT scans. I started getting dizzy a lot and had these terrible headaches. But by the time it showed up on the scans, it was already at stage four. They are going to operate next week, but my chances…" She shrugged.

Compassion swelled for the poor woman. "I've seen what the surgeons do. Best you not let them anywhere near you." Anxiety spiked. "Especially not inside your head!"

Strangely, she laughed. "There have been quite a few advancements, you know." She wrinkled her nose. "Sanitation, for one."

Self-aware, he took a step away from her. He'd done his best to keep his face and hands clean, but it had been a week since Peggy had boiled his uniform.

"What's your name, anyway?"

"I'm Sergeant Caleb Dockery."

"Lena."

He startled. Did she expect him to address her by her Christian name after they'd only just met? He gestured toward the door. "*Miss Lowrey*, if you please, I would like to assist you in finding your way home."

The lady shook her head, but seemed unsure. "I don't know if I can get back by going that way."

The muscles in his jaw constricted, and he could hear his fellows in the hallway chuckling. Just what he needed. He let out a slow breath.

"My best chance to wake up from this dream is to go back to bed." She brightened, though she appeared to be trying to convince herself as much as him. "Then I will wake up back in the real world."

"Real world?"

She nodded, turning back toward the bed. "Yes, I think—"

Her words were cut off by a sudden series of shouts from below. Caleb turned and rushed out the door, the woman scurrying on his heels. In the upper hall, men that could stand scrambled toward the railing to look over.

"Lawd have mercy! He bleedin' all over the floor!"

Caleb leaned over the railing, though he couldn't get a good look at the hall below. It must be another botched surgery.

Pink nails clutched his sleeve. "What's going on?"

He turned to answer, but before he could utter a word, Miss Lowrey hurried off in a flurry of yellow ruffles.

Chapter Four

*G*ood gravy. She'd never escape this nightmare. How was she supposed to sleep in order to get her mind to wake up when people were screaming in the house?

Lena barreled down the stairs, nearly tripping on the ridiculously long skirts. Really, how did women function in these things? She reached the bottom of the stairs, where chaos erupted.

Men shouted, pushing others away from the door that led into the parlor, the room directly across the foyer from the library.

"Someone hold that man down!" A man's voice boomed over the myriad of others. "And someone get more rags to stop the bleeding!"

Her heart leapt. Well, this might be a dream, but at least here she could help.

Lena elbowed her way into what she expected to be a grisly scene. The room adjacent to the parlor, the dining room, had been turned into a makeshift operating room. The doctor—the man who'd scowled at her earlier—leaned over a patient without a mask.

Blood spattered his clothing and he screamed at two other soldiers to hold down the flailing man on the table. Instincts kicking in, she rushed to his side.

Prying back the patient's eyelids, Lena shook her head. "He is not properly sedated. You'll have to send him fully under if you have any hope of completing…"—she glanced at the bloody stump the doctor had been sawing on—"completing that amputation." She narrowed her eyes. "And it seems you did not properly ligate a vein, which would account for the profuse bleeding."

The doctor stared at her in astonishment.

"You better hurry, before he bleeds out."

The doctor, his eyes wide above his beard, gaped at her. "Who *is* this woman?"

She ignored him. "Do you at least have chloroform? If memory serves me right, you should have some basics in this time."

He sputtered. "Look here, woman, I have already administered—"

"You haven't administered enough. Now, are you going to continue to argue with me, or would you like me to help you keep this man from dying?" Not bothering to wait for his reply, she turned to a teen holding down the patient.

"You. Dose another rag and hold it over his mouth."

The boy glanced at the doctor but did as she said. In a moment, the patient ceased twitching and lay still.

"I need antimicrobial soap, gloves, scrubs, and…" They had no idea what any of that was. Lena shook her head and started over. "Someone get me an apron and something to wash my hands with."

Peggy shouted something from behind the men crowding the door, and in a moment Lena was presented with clouded water and a sliver of lye soap.

Lena wasted no time scrubbing her hands and arms, muttering to herself about the lack of sanitation. But at least she'd washed her hands. She had doubts the surgeon had done the same. She turned back to him with her head held high. "I am prepared to assist you, doctor."

"Who *are* you?"

"Lena. I'm a nurse. Well, almost, I had to drop out during my last semester."

The hair under his nose twitched. "You've had training?"

"Yes."

"With Nightingale or Dix?"

She cocked her head. "Um…University of Mississippi Medical Center."

The man cursed and bent back over the leg. "Just get a rag and get this blood out of the way. He won't stop bleeding."

Lena leaned over, snatching a rag without even looking to see who proffered it. "Here's your problem," she said, pointing to where blood welled in the ragged flesh. "You didn't ligate the saphenous vein properly. That's where the blood is coming from."

He mumbled another curse and dug his fingers around in the serrated tissue. Finally, he located the vein, looped a thread around it, and pulled it closed.

Lena almost asked where he'd gotten the suture, which looked like common sewing thread, but thought better of it.

For the next hour, she fell into a rhythm she had nearly forgotten, once again feeling useful as she turned her focus on a patient who needed her care. Finally, the doctor leaned back, stretching the muscles in his shoulders, and surprisingly, turned the final stitches over to her.

Lena made careful, practiced loops, pulling together the folds of skin over the stump of the man's right leg. "What caused the need for amputation?"

"Gangrene," the doctor said with a grunt, already heading for the door.

She winced. She'd remembered reading how many men died simply because they did not have proper antibiotics and clean facilities. She could help with that. Teach them about disinfecting and…

What was she thinking? This was all a dream. An escape her mind conjured to make her feel useful again. Somewhere in the recesses of her heart, she must be more upset than she'd thought about having to cut her schooling short.

"You did amazing work."

The feminine voice drew Lena's attention as she washed her hands in the basin. The girl who'd yelled at her earlier now stood solemnly in the doorway, watching her. She fidgeted with the cuff on her sleeve. "Why didn't you tell me you were a nurse?"

Lena shrugged. "I guess I didn't think it mattered." She wiped her hands on a clean portion of the rag and turned to one of the soldiers—really a boy who shouldn't even be out of high school yet—and instructed him to have the patient moved to a bed.

"You didn't think having trained as a nurse would be important in a hospital?" The girl stepped aside as the men hefted the patient with minimal care and hauled him away.

Lena barked a laugh. "I thought I was at a bed-and-breakfast." She walked over to the girl, who appeared no more than sixteen or seventeen, then glanced in the direction the teenage boy had gone. They seemed so young to be dealing with all of this. At sixteen, Lena's biggest problem had been figuring out what to wear to the movies with her friends.

Compassion swelled. This poor girl had a house full of dying soldiers.

"So," Lena said. "Where are your parents?"

The girl tucked a strand of blond hair back into her bun. "Both have passed. My grandfather by marriage is on his way to take up residence with me."

"And what did you say your name was again?"

"Miss Ross."

Lena made a face. "You want me to call you *Miss Ross?*"

The girl seemed confused. "As I have made your acquaintance just this day, I would say that is proper, *Miss Lowrey.*"

Lena couldn't help but laugh again. "Whatever you say." She lifted her shoulders. "But you can call me Lena. Everyone does."

The teen tipped her head to the side. "If you insist." She frowned. "I am still concerned about how you came to be at Rosswood. But as it seems you are an answer to prayer, I shall not further question it. Perhaps you are an angel sent to aid us."

Was she joking? Of all the harebrained… "No. I'm just me. I wish I could tell you how I got here, but I can't. Though I am willing to help you." She shrugged. "At least for as long as I'm here. Maybe that'll be enough."

The girl didn't return Lena's smile. "Then perhaps we should get you into a more suitable gown, and you can help me with the evening ministrations."

Lena shrugged. What else did she have to do?

Caleb kept his eyes on the cards, but his mind drifted to the strange woman below. What was she doing down there? Was she in trouble? He contemplated going to see for himself, but each time the idea surfaced, he turned it aside. What business was it of his what a madwoman did?

He clenched the cards, tension radiating up his arm and into his shoulder. At the sound of footsteps he folded his cards over and stood.

"Now what?" Sergeant Wells grumbled. "I'd have better luck with a Blue Belly than with you."

Caleb ignored him, straightening his jacket and waiting at the top of the stairs as the women approached. Miss Ross gave him a nod, not seeming perturbed with his lack of progress with removing Miss Lowrey.

Miss Lowrey offered him a brilliant smile that sent a shock of heat through his chest. Her warm gaze slid over him, then snagged on the bandage on his head. She paused as she approached him, leaning close enough that he could smell a faint scent of…strawberries?

"Hmm. I'd like to take a look at that."

Caleb glanced at Miss Ross.

"It would seem Miss Lowrey has trained as a nurse. She offered pertinent aid to Major Thrasher."

Miss Lowrey grinned but it reminded him of the sly look the boys gave when they won a round.

His brow scrunched beneath his wrappings.

"It seems," Miss Lowrey said, chin lifted, "that my training has come as quite a shock to everyone."

How could he tell which things she said were true and which were fantasies? But if she fabricated such an important truth, surely Major Thrasher would have noticed and expelled her from the proceedings.

As he contemplated, she reached up and tugged on his wrappings, unhindered by the thoughts of common courtesy.

He stepped back. "It is not a pretty sight."

"I'm sure I've seen worse." She pointed to a chair against the wall. "Sit."

The boys chuckled now, and he could feel heat rising into his ears. Still, curiosity uprooted his better senses, and he followed her orders.

She pulled the wrappings free, and he expected her to gasp, or at least stiffen at the sight of what had once been his eye. Even Miss Ross, whom he'd seen tend all manner of wounds, had been unable to completely hide her disgust.

This woman didn't even flinch.

"It looks like you have some tissue necrosis." She poked at him.

"What?"

She leaned back. "Follow my finger, please."

Sticking a finger in the air, she slowly moved it back and forth in front of his face. He traced the strange pink nail with his good eye for a moment, then flicked his gaze to her face.

A smooth complexion, dusted with the slightest spray of freckles one would never notice unless beholding her up close. Still, not the sheltered coloring of the genteel. Perhaps with her training she'd spent time in field hospitals. Of course. That could explain her placid reaction to his injury.

"There is deadened tissue here. It will need to be removed, and you need antibiotics."

"I'll not have one of them cutting any more on my eye," Caleb said, leaning as far away from her as he could manage.

"But you need…" She stopped, frowning. "I see your point, yes."

Miss Lowrey called for Miss Ross to bring her some clean linens, seeming to have no problem giving her hostess orders.

She knelt in front of him, and his pulse quickened. Thankfully, she didn't seem to notice as she studied him while Miss Ross relayed the instructions to Peggy. Miss

Lowrey tapped her finger on her chin, then brightened.

"Oh! I know!" She leapt to her feet, surprising them all. "Vinegar!" She seemed pleased with herself. "That'll do it."

"What now?" Peggy asked, putting her hands on her hips. "What you want with vinegar?"

"It's acetic acid, which will work as an antiseptic in a pinch."

The other two women stared at her. Good. Didn't seem like they knew what she was talking about either.

Miss Lowrey shook her head, throwing a glance to the ceiling. "It keeps the infection away. Won't let them get gangrene." She pointed at Caleb. "We'll start with him, but I suspect most of them will need it."

Sergeant Wells let out a whoop. "You goin' to let that madwoman pour vinegar in your eye?"

Caleb shot him a hard glance, and Wells quieted. He looked back at Miss Lowrey, the exposure of his bad eye making him uncomfortable. "I'd rather not, thank you."

She frowned at him. "Don't be ridiculous. You need treatment."

He kept his tone even, though they had gained the attention of all seven men taking up residence in the upper hall. "I will yield to washing and wrapping, Miss Lowrey, but you'll not test out your absurd imaginings on me."

Miss Lowrey bristled, and Sergeant Wells let out a low whistle. She narrowed her eyes at the soldier watching them and he quieted, looking away. She turned back to Caleb with a flat stare. "Well, if you refuse treatment, it's not my concern."

She rose and turned away. "Miss Ross? You said something about another gown?"

Miss Ross blinked rapidly, then pointed to her bed-chamber. Miss Lowrey snatched up her skirts and marched toward the door.

The nerve of that man! Just because he didn't understand it didn't mean he should refuse good care. She stomped into the room, unsure exactly why she was so angry. Maybe because this was *her* dream, and he should have done what she'd suggested.

Lena rubbed her temples. What a stupid thought.

"Are you well, Miss Lowrey?" Miss Ross came closer, the older woman on her heels.

Peggy sighed. "Maybe all that excitement done give her the flutters again, Miss Belle."

Ah. So the girl's name was Belle. Strange how the older woman called the younger *Miss Belle.* "I don't have flutters." She lowered her hands. "In fact, I feel better than I have in a long time."

The girl smiled. "That's good, is it not?"

"Sure, Belle. But since this is just a dream, why would I give myself a headache?"

"Dream?"

"Belle?"

The two women spoke at once, both frowning. Peggy pointed a finger at Lena. "Who say you could call her Belle? Ain't nobody but me and her momma call her that."

Lena sighed. "That's not her name?"

"My name is Annabelle Ross. Belle is a name of affection those closest to me use, *Miss Lowrey*."

Lena didn't miss the jab but chose to ignore it. Who would have thought names would be such a big ordeal? "Look, I'm not used to being so formal with teenagers. How about you call me Lena and I'll call you Annabelle." She gestured to the older woman. "Same for you. Peggy, right?"

Peggy shook her head. "Somethin' plumb wrong with this one, Miss Belle."

Annabelle chose not to answer, and instead walked over to a carved wardrobe against the wall. Lena looked closer. Wasn't that the same one from her room back at…well, at the *other* Rosswood?

Annabelle pulled an item from the wardrobe. "This should fit you well enough." She held out a brown dress peppered with little white flowers.

Lena took it, feeling silly. What was she doing?

"We will leave you to change," Annabelle said, turning toward the door. She paused with her hand on the knob, lips pressed together. Then she seemed to come to a decision. "While you do, I will see if we have any vinegar. We shall test your idea."

Peggy muttered something, but followed Annabelle out of the door, leaving Lena alone. She stood there for a time, staring at the long dress in her hands. It looked real. The rough spin of the fabric with the slightly uneven stitches made by hand *seemed* real.

Her throat tightened. *Oh, Lord. What is happening to me?*

She closed her eyes and waited, but the sounds of men's laughter in the hall didn't fade, nor did the feel of the dress in her hands dissipate. She should get in the bed and close her eyes. Will herself to wake up in the right time. But...she did want to see if the vinegar worked. And for some reason, she really wanted to prove herself to that surly soldier. A dream would end when it ended. In the meantime, she'd make the most of it.

Finally, Lena huffed, freed the buttons behind her neck, and pulled the yellow gown over her head.

Chapter Five

"*L*ena, darling, are you awake?"

She bolted upright, the pain in her head throbbing. "Momma?"

Momma held her hand, the smile pulling her lips faltering. "Of course. Who else would it be?"

Sighing, Lena closed her eyes. "I keep having these dreams. Strange, vivid dreams that seem so real."

Silence settled over them. Perhaps Lena shouldn't have added to Momma's burden, but she deserved to know. If something happened and they had to go back to the hospital, it would need to be added to her list of symptoms.

"We have no way of knowing how the tumor will affect your brain," Momma said, picking up on Lena's unspoken train of thought. She patted Lena's arm where it lay across a beautifully worked quilt. "The doctor said you could smell strange things, or see colors in your line of vision. Perhaps more active dreaming occurs as well." Momma leaned closer. "Are they bad dreams?"

"Well, no," Lena said drawing her knees to her

chest. "Not exactly, I guess. I keep dreaming that I go back in time to this house during the Civil War. It's a hospital, and there are wounded men here."

Momma seemed relieved. "Probably because we listened to the history of the house. Maybe we can talk about them. It might be fun to see what you think the past might have looked like."

Lena swung her legs down from the bed. "Yes, I thought the same." Never mind she'd dreamed up a hospital *before* she found out the history of the house. "It just seemed so…real."

After a trip to the bathroom to splash cool water on her face, they returned downstairs and set out to try the restaurant Mr. Hylander suggested. The drive was a short one and brought them to a quaint old general store with wood railings and old tin signs.

The screen door slammed as a young family exited, a little girl tugging on her mother's hand and pointing to some kind of trinket in her hand. Lena smiled at them, feeling an odd pinch in her heart. Before her diagnosis, she thought she still had plenty of time. Now that she knew she would likely never have a family, it chafed more than she'd expected. Lena looked away. Annoyed tears could be brought on so easily.

She followed Momma inside, immediately struck by the smells of Southern cooking. They waited with other patrons who crowded the entry. The out-of-the-way place seemed to draw tourists, who were probably on their way to the Natchez fall pilgrimage. And Lena could see why. The place was a novelty of sorts, certainly different than any other place she'd been. The walls were lined with antiques of every variety, and a collection of tables had been strewn through the middle as if the owner wasn't entirely sure what sort of business he meant to run.

An older man greeted them, his smile bright as he directed them to a table. They took their seats.

"This is the best fried chicken you'll ever eat," he proclaimed, his smile wide underneath a broad nose and joyful brown eyes.

Lena nodded absently. "That so?"

The man didn't seem to notice as he hurried to the next set of guests, smiling and directing them to another mismatched table.

"We'll see for ourselves, won't we?" Momma's voice held the hint of laughter that soothed the soul as sweetly as the delicious scents permeating the air stirred Lena's hunger.

She let herself relax. No use thinking about dreams she couldn't change and spoil the fun of the evening.

After a nice lady took their drink order, they chose the buffet option and rounded a corner to an adjacent room, where the tantalizing aroma swelled to mouth-watering heights. The same man who had greeted them at the door directed them to the food, telling them about his mother's recipe.

Lena found him charming and offered a genuine smile.

With heaping plates, they returned to their table. The chicken really was delicious, the skin crisp and the meat tender, and Lena ate more than she had in some time, which seemed to please Momma tremendously.

While they waited for dessert, Lena excused herself to go to the restroom.

The hall leading away from the dining area toward the restrooms was just as odd as the rest of the place. It looked more like an old mercantile untouched by the modern era than it did like the restaurant it was supposed to be. People had pinned their business cards to the wall, and as she wandered further down the winding hall, she realized the farther she went, the more the cards had colored with age.

Pictures in dusty frames hung everywhere, depicting people in shabby dresses and worn boots with stoic expressions. Depression era, if she had to guess. Lena lingered, letting her eyes roam down the collection of cards and photographs. She ignored the restroom and kept moving deeper into the winding hall, following the trail of aging photographs. As the din of the restaurant faded, the aroma of home cooking gave way to the dusty perfume of forgotten memories.

Above her, antique plow yokes and rusty farming equipment hung from the ceiling. What an odd place. A moment of panic surged. She hadn't wandered off into another dream world, had she? Lena shook the thought off. She hadn't passed out or fallen asleep. Still, the hairs on the back of her neck rose and the tingle of intangible anticipation clung to her nerves.

A larger frame caught her eye, and Lena stepped past age-tinted photographs to see what the larger one near the end of this hall of memories contained. She came to a stop in front of it, and her heart skipped.

Though covered in dust, the frame was still flecked

with gilded paint. It surrounded a sepia-colored depiction of a large porch flanked with massive columns.

Rosswood.

There on the porch stood a woman in a wide gown holding a toddler on her hip. Next to her, a large man with broad shoulders rested a protective hand on the woman's shoulder. Both had light hair and features. Beside them, another couple smiled, the woman's dark hair piled thickly on her head but still spilling down over her shoulder. In front of the couple were two children, a boy and a girl.

Lena looked back to the first couple. Something about them seemed familiar. She leaned closer, and then took her forearm to smear the dust from the glass. Another figure emerged a few feet from the two couples...an African-American woman with wide lips and a generous nose, her hands clasped in front of her.

Lena peered closer and gasped. It couldn't be. She narrowed her eyes and looked to the first couple, her nose now only inches from the glass. The woman who looked back at her had aged from the teenager in her dreams, but was unmistakable.

Annabelle Ross.

Lena squeezed her eyes closed, trying to clear her vision. Impossible! She'd never seen a picture of this girl. How, then, did she look exactly the same as Lena had dreamed her? She looked back to the woman who resembled Peggy. No mistaking that hers was the very same face that looked at Lena with contempt each time she trespassed into the wrong Rosswood.

Heart hammering, Lena stepped back from the photograph, suddenly frightened. Did she now see things in her waking hours as well? What was reality? She stood there in the empty hall, hands shaking, and then sprinted back the other direction. She passed a startled woman waiting for the restroom and bounded back out into the din of the restaurant, grasping for the hard lines of the here and now.

Chest heaving, she scurried to the safety of Momma's side and dropped into her chair.

"You all right?" Momma's eyes widened.

Lena forced herself to slow her breathing. "They make the bathroom a difficult thing to find."

Momma stared at her a moment but said nothing more even though her eyes never strayed from Lena's face as she sipped her tea.

After several moments to regain her calm, Lena tested her grasp on reality. "I saw an old photograph back there of Rosswood."

"Really?" Momma hardly seemed surprised.

"Yes. There were people standing on the porch. Two couples, some children, and another woman."

Momma set down her tea. "I wonder if it's the same people Mr. Hylander told us about."

"I think it was Annabelle Ross and Peggy, but I don't know who the others were."

"Peggy?" Momma shook her head. "No, dear. That's the lady who works there now. She's going to make breakfast in the morning." Concern edged her tone.

Lena laughed, but it sounded forced even to her

own ears. "Oh, not that Peggy. The...." She lifted her shoulders. "The other one."

"Other one?"

"The one from my dream."

Momma's brow creased. "I don't understand."

Lena leaned back in her chair. "Neither do I."

A woman brought two bowls of banana pudding to the table, and then the same older man who had greeted them and directed them to the buffet called for everyone's attention. Dressed in simple slacks and a button-down shirt, he had a mannerism of one who was comfortable in anything he wore.

Expressive eyes danced underneath a head full of coarse dark hair dusted in white. He smiled at them, clearly happy to be there, and then broke into a soulful song that brought the crowd to silence. His rich voice washed over them, and by the time the song finished, the people all watched with rapture.

They applauded the man called Mr. D, paid for their meal, and got back in the Volkswagen. It took three cranks, but the engine in the back finally caught.

No sooner had they pulled from the parking lot than Momma said, "Tell me more about this photograph you saw."

Of course Momma wouldn't have forgotten that. Lena shouldn't have said anything. "Oh, it was hanging back there with a bunch of other stuff. Looked like Rosswood with the porch columns, but I guess it could have been any of these old houses."

Momma cut on the blinker onto Red Lick Road. "You said it was Annabelle Ross and Peggy. Are you certain?"

"No." Lena leaned her head back and closed her eyes. The car jostled underneath her as it rumbled down the rough road, causing her head to bounce. She opened her eyes. "It was a blonde woman in a big dress. I assumed it had to be Annabelle Ross, since she used to live in that house."

Momma nodded, though Lena could sense her concern. Determined to speak of other things, Lena fished around for another idea. "After my surgery, where do you want to go next?"

"What do you mean?"

"Let's plan a trip to go somewhere once I get out of the hospital. It'll give us something to look forward to."

Momma brightened, and for the remainder of the drive they threw out wild ideas of all the places they would love to see, both ignoring the financial impossibility of ever seeing them or the fact that Lena might not make it out of the hospital after her surgery. But it made for good laughter, and as they returned to the house and sat in the library for another three hours, their laughter turned to simply enjoying one another's company and remembering good times.

Finally, somewhere around midnight, Momma's eyes became too heavy for her to continue to hide.

"Get some rest, Momma. We still have all day tomorrow."

Momma rose and stretched. "You're not coming?"

"I took a long nap, remember? I think I'll stay up a little while and look at those diary pages Mr. Hylander told us about." At Momma's look of concern, she added, "I'll bring them upstairs and sit on that little couch outside our room."

Lena gathered the laminated pages, turned off the light, and followed Momma up the staircase. Momma kissed her cheek goodnight, and Lena promised not to stay up too late and tire herself out. Once Momma went into their room, Lena plucked out the thought she'd tried to bury all evening.

What if it hadn't been a dream? Impossible, of course. But...

She flipped through the diary pages, but they'd been written by a man, and mostly contained cotton numbers and the goings-on at the house before the Civil War. She found nothing about Annabelle or Peggy.

Lena went downstairs to return the pages and scanned the books along the massive library shelves Mr. Hylander planned to replace. How long had they been there? Some of the books seemed ancient. Struck by an idea, Lena snagged a piece of paper from a pad on the rolltop desk, wrote a quick note, and signed her name. Then she returned to the shelf to find a likely specimen. But in which of them would she be able to hide the paper without it being discovered over the course of more than a century and a half?

Shaking her head at her absurdity, Lena nevertheless continued to look for a shard of the impossible. Perhaps the books wouldn't work. It would need to be a place where no one would think to look. But where? She wandered around the library, then to the dimly lit parlor and dining room across the hall, and finally made her way up the stairs with the scrap of pure foolishness still clutched in her hand.

But she had to know.

She lingered in the upper hall, listening to a frog bleat its call to another of its kind. Her gaze drifted to the carved frame surrounding the door to the upper balcony. Trying not to let herself think too much on her insanity, Lena folded the paper into a narrow strip and knelt by the jamb.

There. The wooden frame had a small gap at the base where frame, wall, and floor molding met. Wiggling it back and forth, Lena wedged the paper in. There. Now she could see...

She sat back on her heels. See what? The paper wouldn't be in the past, because she'd put it there now. No, she had to go back and hide it then, and then come back and check it now.

Ignoring the fact she sounded like a character from Dr. Suess, Lena rose and stood there quietly, contemplating all she knew about what had happened, trying to loosely apply her schooling to a very different situation. As a nursing student, she had to look at the manifestation of symptoms, and deduce what had caused the condition.

So, what order of events had occurred? First, she'd put on the dress and become dizzy. Then she'd appeared in the past. She went to take off the dress, passed out on the floor, then awoke back in her normal clothes in the correct time.

The dress, then. It had to be the link. She looked toward the door where she and Momma shared a room.

But she'd not put on the dress when she took a nap. She'd fallen asleep in the bed, then awoken in the same bed in eighteen sixty-four...again wearing the yellow dress. So not just the dress. And how had she come out of the dream the last time?

She'd taken off the dress to change it to the brown one. She glanced at the door again. Did she dare succumb to this craziness? In doing so, would she only push herself further into a place she might never break free from?

Lena hesitated only a moment longer, then strode to the room. She cracked open the door and heard Momma's soft snores. Before she could talk herself out of it, she made her way through the dim room and to the wardrobe. She caught sight of her shadowed features in the mirror, the hall light giving just enough illumination for her to see the deep circles under her eyes. Eyes that held the truth of her condition, eyes that knew she would soon end her days without having really done anything with them.

Why had God allowed her to nearly complete her nurse's training, but then end her time on earth before she could even use it?

My ways are not your ways, and my thoughts are not your thoughts. The verse surfaced unbidden, and she pushed it away. If only she had another chance.

She opened the wardrobe door, half expecting the dress to be gone, but it flowed from the hanger with a cascade of daffodil ruffles as though it were the yellow-brick road meant to take her back to her own strange version of Oz.

After pulling it from the hanger and bunching it in her arms, Lena crept back through the room and into the hall. Before she could tell herself to do otherwise, she thrust her arms under the skirt and slithered the gown over her head.

Immediately, the world flooded with light again. Lena yelped and jumped back, finding herself exactly where she'd last been in the dream. She still clutched the brown dress in one hand, but in the other....

She opened her fist. A small folded paper rested within. So she'd brought it back with her. What other things could she bring?

A knock sounded at the door. "Miss Lowrey? Are you ready?"

Lena smiled and tossed the brown dress down on the bed.

Chapter Six

Caleb flexed his hands, studying the calloused places that had formed on his palms and the pads of his thumb and forefinger. He'd never had the refined hands of a gentleman, but the thickened skin he'd developed from his labor in his father's shop didn't compare to the rough scales gained by digging trenches and robbing lives.

His hand of cards forgotten and turned over to Jenkins, Caleb rose and ventured to the door to the balcony. A breath of air would do him some good. At least, that's what he told himself even as his feet slowed and he lingered by the open door to Miss Ross's chamber.

"You cannot mean to wear that gown while working." Miss Ross's voice held a mixture of annoyance and disbelief.

"I don't expect you to understand," Miss Lowrey quipped, "but I can't seem to wear a different one." Her voice was deeper than most ladies', though not in an unfeminine way. Instead, it seemed to glide over him like warm silk.

Caleb frowned, untangling the caress of her voice from the words she spoke. Why could she not don a different garment? Odd woman. She had assisted the surgeon and spoke as one who had taken schooling, yet seemed at a loss with simple things like addressing acquaintances properly and wearing the appropriate clothing for the occasion.

And Caleb found himself intrigued. He stepped to the door. "All is well?"

Miss Lowrey, her brown eyes bright and luminous and her face that of one who was accustomed to having her say, turned to address him. "As you can see, we are in the middle of a conversation."

Miss Ross startled, her cheeks reddening at the lady's tone.

He studied the bold woman standing there with her chin held high. He searched her features, looking for the clue that would lead him to the piece he knew he must be missing from this mystery. What kind of woman was both brazen and used to having others under her instruction? Yet at the same time seemed at a loss for proper mannerisms and lacked the charm of a lady born to...

His gut tightened. Of course. Why hadn't he seen it? His brother had warned of such women, who came to speak in the place of husbands and fathers, women who fancied themselves like men in a world of business.

His mind worked quickly, unraveling the threads even as she moved to leave without awaiting his reply. Why would a woman, likely a suffragette type and probably from the North, suddenly appear at a Confederate hospital? The answer was as sure as it was alarming.

Spy.

He stepped closer, blocking her path. "Miss Lowrey, you are continuing to cause a rumpus in this hospital. It would not be inappropriate to have you removed from it. Especially if you cannot give due cause for being here."

Miss Ross frowned. "What say you, Sergeant?"

"I say if we were somewhere other than a hospital and a stranger showed up with a thin tale of where they came from, and with no reason for why they should be there, and if such a person asked a great deal of questions..."

Miss Lowrey's brow scrunched in confusion. An act, surely.

It was Peggy who spoke, her words coming out in a gasp. "You think she be a spy!"

Miss Ross shook her head. "Nonsense." She gestured at Miss Lowrey. "Clearly she is a woman."

"As is Rose Greenhow."

Miss Ross pressed her lips together. "Those tales are merely speculation."

"Oh, come on." Miss Lowrey rolled her eyes dramatically. "I'm not some kind of spy."

"Then who are you?" Caleb asked, stepping even closer.

"I told you."

"Where are your loyalties in this war?"

She squared her shoulders. "Loyalties? I have no

loyalties in a war that ended…" She pinched the bridge of her nose. "Oh, never mind."

"You must have loyalties, Miss Lowrey. Be it to North or South?"

She stared at him, taking longer to answer than he would have liked. "I am from Mississippi. I was born here."

"And?"

Miss Ross shifted her weight from one foot to the other, clearly distressed. The lady's maid stood near the wall, watching them all with keen eyes that did not often stay lowered. Caleb waited, letting the air grow thick with the weight of Miss Lowrey's contemplation.

"Oh, good gravy. This is ridiculous. I am *not* a spy. I don't even care about your war." She moved to push past him. "Now, if you will excuse me, I have something to do."

He snagged her wrist. "I think not."

She thrust her hand forward and made a sharp turn of her hand, circling his arm back and snapping his hold on her. Her eyes flashed at him. "Don't do that again."

Shocked, he watched her stomp out of the room. Had he just been outmaneuvered by a woman?

These people were crazy! A spy? Really? She hiked up the dress tangling her legs and stepped around a man lying on the floor. The soldier sputtered something, but she ignored him. This was stupid. She shouldn't be trying to do this. But by this point it was either find out the truth or risk what little sanity she had left.

All she had to do was put the paper in the hiding place. Simple. She reached the door to the upper balcony and then paused, her wits finally speaking over her frustration. She clutched the paper tighter and opened the door instead, stepping out onto the balcony.

If these paranoid people saw her stick a piece of paper in a slot in the wall, they would most surely snatch it free to see what she had done. Lena crossed the porch and splayed her hands on the rail. What happened to her, well, the *real* her when she came here? Was her body actually simultaneously back in her time?

Her heart hammered. Would Momma think her dead? No, likely just asleep. Or in a coma. She scrubbed a hand down her face. Then might Momma rush her to a hospital? What would happen if her mind was in 1864 while her body was moved from Rosswood? Would she end up out in the middle of nowhere where a modern hospital hadn't yet been built?

"Miss Lowrey!" The intense soldier burst through the door, the scowl on his face all the more fearsome for the bandage over his eye.

She groaned. "What do you want?"

He paused as though she had slapped him. "I want to know the truth."

Lena turned back to look out over the field that splayed forth from the house, a great swath of land stuck through with dead cotton stalks. "No, you don't. What you really want is for me to make up something you would find believable."

He came to stand at her side, his presence formidable and confident...and not at all like the men, well, boys really, she knew back home. She shifted away from him, alarmed at the thought.

"I assure you, Miss Lowrey, I do but require the truth. If you are capable of giving it."

Was she? Could she tell him her fractured mind was splintering? Or, worse, that she might actually believe God had heard her plea and had taken her tumor away...but only in the past? She closed her eyes. She wouldn't believe that tale either. But if she couldn't tell a figment of her imagination—even just a man from the past she would never see again—then who else could she share the burden with?

"I'm not a spy, uh...what was your name again?"

"Sergeant Dockery."

She sighed. "That's not what I mean."

"Then what do you mean?" His voice edged with implications.

Why was he toying with her? She let sarcasm thicken her tone. "So your parents named you *Sergeant?*"

"Pardon?" He rubbed a hand across the back of his neck. "You are by far the most confounding woman I have ever met."

She suddenly laughed as the confusion softening his features made her realize how attractive he was, even with his damaged eye. Not handsome in that refined and metro way of the guys back home, but in a rugged and manly way that stirred....

Lena cut off the bizarre thought and shook her head. "Sorry." She scooted away from him. "I meant, what is your actual first name again? I'm afraid I've forgotten." Which happened a lot lately.

He tilted his head to the side, an odd combination of fearsome biker-guy and lost puppy. "My first name? As in my Christian name?"

"Christian name?"

"The primary one given me by my parents." He squared his broad shoulders. "The name that precedes my surname."

She thought a hint of humor laced his tone, but she couldn't be sure. "Uh, yeah. That one." She plucked at a hangnail.

"Caleb."

"I'm Lena." She shifted her weight, overly aware of this looming man who studied her with such intensity. "Well, Amberlena Elizabeth, but that's a mouthful if ever there was one, so I just go by Lena." Dummy. Now she was rambling! She eased a little farther away. "You don't have to keep calling me Miss Lowrey like I'm in some beauty pageant."

"Beauty pageant?"

"Never mind." She shook her head. "Look, I know you people like to be formal and all, but it just feels weird to keep calling everyone *Miss* this and *Mister* that. It's silly. Just call me Lena, okay?"

He seemed startled and then shook his head. "I will not let you distract me from what I came to learn, *Miss Lowrey*."

The truth. Well, she'd like to know the truth herself, wouldn't she? She squeezed the paper in her hand. "You wouldn't understand."

He moved closer, a slight breeze brushing his sandy hair across his brow. "Give me the opportunity."

"I don't know you."

"And that matters to speak the truth?"

She peered up at him, his earnest expression tempting her to speak the words aloud. In so doing, she would risk opening herself. But then, what did it matter? She sucked in a breath. "I'm from the future."

Caleb set his jaw against the seething anger threatening to break free. She mocked him! "You think me a fool?"

Disappointment flicked in her eyes, as though she'd actually thought he would believe such an outrageous fabrication. Did she truly think him witless because he could see her with only one eye?

"You asked for the truth. I gave it. It's not up to me if you believe it."

The words grated across him, tearing open a half scabbed-over wound. He reached out and gripped her shoulder. "Who are you? Why speak those words?"

"What?" Her eyes widened, and she whipped her arm around, instantly breaking his hold. She stepped back away from him, wary.

"Who told you to speak those words? Who do you know?"

She slowly eased closer to the door, her chest rising and falling quickly. "You're crazy! You asked for the truth. I gave it to you. I know it sounds insane—believe me, I do. But I can't help it!"

He moved closer again, his lip twitching. "You came here seeking me out. He told you to say those words. Where is he?"

"He who?"

"Do not play games!"

He reached for her again, but she darted around him, tripping on her skirts and nearly falling to the ground. She righted herself and snatched her gown clear above her knees, exposing long, slender legs and smooth thighs. The suddenness of the sight stopped his thrust forward.

She slipped through the door and slammed it behind her. Vexing woman! She'd planned that! He yanked the door back open, and his quick strides carried him through the upper hall even as her shorter ones bounded away like a doe.

Someone shouted, and men lurched to their feet, but Caleb merely pushed past them. One man bumped into his side and he stumbled, cursing the missing eye that made it difficult to perceive the location of objects.

He rushed down the stairs after her, focused on a flair of yellow ruffles flying out behind her. The doctor shouted at him, and just in time, his mind snapped free of the vixen's hold to remind him that a superior officer had commanded him.

Caleb stopped and threw a hasty salute. "Sir! The spy escapes."

Miss Lowrey stopped at the front door, her eyes bulging. "I'm not a spy!" She gestured at Caleb. "And that man tried to grab me."

Major Thrasher scowled. "What does this woman speak of?"

Caleb refused to look at her. "I have good cause to believe that woman is a Yankee spy."

"I am not!"

Miss Ross came down the stairs, her controlled movements the exact opposite of the mystery standing at the front door. "What is this about, gentlemen?"

"It seems Sergeant Dockery believes Miss Lowrey a spy." Major Thrasher rocked back on his heels and stared at Caleb for a moment, then leaned near and spoke so only he could hear. "I do not wish to disregard any reliable information, but you and I both know you are a bit more sensitive to such matters. Do you think it possible you are seeing more than is there?"

Some of the anger fled from his chest. Did he? Did he see the one responsible for Sam's death even in a frightened woman?

Major Thrasher clasped his shoulder. "Let us keep a close eye on her, shall we? But all the same, her skills are valuable to me here."

His brothers in arms could use all the care they could get, and the vixen had apparently proved her worth with medical skills to have so quickly gained Major Thrasher's approval. "Yes, sir." He saluted. Then, without looking at the strange woman again, he turned toward the staircase.

Chapter Seven

*L*ena heaved, anger warring with the oddest desire to follow the confounding soldier and reassure him. Why should she care what he did? But something about the way pain had flickered in his eye when he seemed to think someone had sent her…

Well, this entire situation just kept getting stranger.

"Miss?"

Realizing the doctor had spoken to her, she pulled her gaze away from the stairs and settled it on the man in front of her. She'd seen the look before. Despite his effort to hide it, exhaustion manifested in the lines around his eyes and the tenseness of his shoulders.

"Yes, doctor?"

"Will you make rounds?"

She studied him, once again wondering just how much training the man actually had. If she taught him a few things, explained the necessity of simple actions like washing tools between surgeries, might she save lives? Help them? Perhaps this entire thing was so that she could serve some purpose, and when it was done, she would be sent back home.

Before she could think better of it, the words slipped free. "Yes. Of course." What harm would it do to teach them a few things while she waited for an opportunity to stash her paper?

The relief in his eyes warmed her even as he gruffly said, "Then you best get to it."

Lena shoved aside her emotions. Time to get to work. Without the headaches and the dizziness, her brain functioned quickly, recalling all the items she would likely need to gather. Anesthetics, if she could find any, bandages, and…

"Why you still in that gown if you be plannin' on working?"

The sharp words brought Lena's thoughts to a halt. How long had Peggy been standing there, watching her? She seemed to appear out of the woodwork.

Peggy narrowed her eyes, assessing Lena with suspicion.

She smoothed her features. What answer would make sense to these people? "I will wear an apron over it. I do not wish to further tax your…lady by wearing her clothing."

The older woman grunted, but something like respect flashed in her eyes just before she turned away. "Well, all right then. I'll get you an apron."

For the next several hours, Lena almost forgot she had a brain tumor. She had more energy than she'd possessed in months, and the work brought a fulfillment she thought to never experience again. She'd been close to becoming an ER nurse, but even without a license, she could be useful here.

From what she remembered of history, little as it was, by this point in the war the people were running low on food and supplies. How many other places were in dire need of care? And though the war would end a few months from now, there would be people in need for years to come.

Lena pulled her thoughts from the vastness of the situation and focused instead on what she could do, one patient at a time. The one before her was a bedraggled man with a scraggly beard and eyes that were nearly vacant. Like the other men she had tended, he seemed worn out and too thin.

"How are you feeling today?" She grasped his wrist to assess his pulse. Strong. She leaned closer and checked his pupils. "On a scale from one to ten, with one feeling great and ten the worst pain of your life, where would you rate your current pain level?"

He blinked. "What now?"

Did they keep charts? She didn't see one. "Your pain level, sir. How is it today?"

"Oh, well, better than yesterday. Didn't cough up no more blood last night."

She stilled. "You've had a lung injury?"

"Ribs are broken."

And may have punctured... "May I assess you?"

He tilted his head. "Doctor already looked at me."

"And I'm sure he did a fine job. He's asked me to make rounds and use my training to help him care for his patients."

The man relaxed a little back into his thin mattress.

"Oh. Well, all right, then."

Lena did what she could, feeling woefully lacking in supplies and equipment but not letting it hinder her. She made him as comfortable as she could with three broken ribs, and then moved to the next man.

By the time the sun started to lower and the light permeating the house waned, she'd made it through all the men in the house. All but one.

Caleb. She had avoided him while seeing to the other men upstairs, even though she'd felt his gaze on her. Why did he think she was a spy? Even as she washed her hands and dried them on a coarse towel, her awareness of him bothered her.

"Have you tended all the men?"

Lena jumped, the sound of Annabelle's sudden voice pulling her from her thoughts.

"Yes." She glanced at Caleb sitting in a chair, arms crossed and looking like a bear in a tattered uniform. "Well, except for Mr. Caleb over there."

She'd meant it lightly, but the girl's eyes widened. Oh. She'd forgotten about the silly name thing again. Why was it such a big deal? But then, in a sea of oddities, why fixate on one ridiculous fish?

Lena brushed her hands down her apron. "Sorry. I mean I've gotten to all the guys except for that sergeant over there."

The teen looked at her as though she wanted to say something, but wouldn't. Instead, she merely tilted her head toward the stairs. "Then I shall go below and assist Peggy with the preparation of our meal."

Lena turned back to the final patient. Seated in a

chair against the wall, Caleb remained still as though he'd been waiting for her. Remembering her professionalism, she made mental notations as she systematically worked through her assessment. He answered each question with detached brevity and waited patiently as she removed his bandage.

The wound didn't seep pus, as many of the other men's wounds had, but it looked more inflamed than she would like. "You still need antiseptic."

He grunted and leaned away from her. "You'll not be pouring vinegar in my eye."

"Of course not." An unexpected smile tugged at the corner of her mouth. "But I will treat the skin left in its place."

The muscles in his jaw twitched. What was wrong with her? She knew better than to try to make light of something like this. The mental grief of losing a body part wasn't something she was supposed to use to try to make a patient relax.

She cleared her throat, trying to return to professional stoicism. "It is merely skin now. It's not as though it will sting your eye."

He leaned away from her.

Well, so much for making things better. "Sorry. I just mean the benefit outweighs the risk."

"I do not understand you."

A smile pulled at her lips again. "That's nothing new. I'm used to it."

"But I want to."

That, she was *not* used to. Her breath caught, her pulse quickening even as she chided herself for it.

"What?"

"I want to understand what your true purpose is here."

Oh. How stupid of her. Why on earth had she thought he meant he wanted to understand her as a person?

He gazed at her with open sincerity, and something strange happened in her stomach. What was it about this burly man that drew her? Perhaps it was his very masculine presence combined with an antiquated refinement that intrigued her. Yeah, that must have been it. She merely found him an interesting point to study in her immersion into another time and culture.

Assuming she hadn't made him up, of course. And if she had, what did that say about her taste in men?

She must have taken too long in answering, because his forehead creased. "Will you tell me?"

Lena rose from where she'd bent before him. "I've already told you, so there's no point in doing it again. I don't understand it any better than you, but it is what it is. Whether you choose to believe it is up to you."

The muscles in his jaw convulsed, and for one brief moment, she wondered what it would be like to smooth the worry from his forehead. Before the thought could better take root, she snatched up her dress and hurried away.

Unfortunately, her tangled emotions came right along with her.

Chapter Eight

*I*t would take but a slip of paper and an unreasonable hope to find the truth. Lena waited until the men who were able went downstairs to eat before she let her fingers caress the object she'd thus far hidden.

The upper hall's single occupant snored enthusiastically, hardly a threat to her mission. She fished the slip of paper out of the little pocket in her dress and caressed it with her thumb. She'd taken too great a risk, staying this long. She'd remained the entire day, which meant it had probably been the entire night back in the real Rosswood. Momma would be getting up soon, and she couldn't let her find Lena's bed empty. Or worse, find her daughter unresponsive.

Certain all was quiet, she squatted and felt around the edge of the doorframe molding. It held together here better than it had when she'd inspected it before. But perhaps if she could find enough of a gap...

"What you be doin' Miss Lowrey?"

Lena spun at Peggy's words, tangling her legs in the mounds of fabric pooling around her and nearly fell over. "Nothing. I had something in my shoe." Never mind the dream had only given her a pair of ankle socks. Why hadn't she thought to put on her Nikes? Next time, she wouldn't forget something so important. She stood and tried to still her shaking fingers before Peggy noticed.

"Supper be on the table." Peggy pointed a finger at her. "If you plan on getting anything to eat, you better get to it."

"I'm fine, thanks."

Peggy put a fist on her hip. "No, ma'am. You need to eat. You worked all day, and I'll not have no little slip of a woman fainting because she was too stubborn to eat."

Lena withheld a groan. Great. They probably had pig brain or something equally inedible in this wretched time. She reluctantly followed Peggy down the stairs and into the same room that had served as a surgery area.

Her stomach flopped. How could they possibly eat here? She mentally added this to the top of her list of changes she would need to discuss with the doctor.

The table had been washed, and chairs that must have been stowed somewhere else were placed around it, but she could not get the image of an operating table out of her mind. Lena placed a finger under her nose, the thought not the only thing turning her stomach. The collection of men thickened the air with the smell of sweat and body odor, a foul aroma that could not be masked by the fragrant platters of food. Bowls were filled with vegetables, and though there seemed to be little meat, the patients would not likely starve. Still, they could do with a more balanced diet. Could she figure out a way to bring them some kind of supplies?

Peggy pointed to a chair next to Annabelle, and Lena begrudgingly made her way fully into the room. Every man in sight pushed his chair back and gained his feet as though she were the Queen of England. Quelling her surprise, she dropped into the chair pulled out for her, if only to more quickly escape the prying eyes of at least ten men. After the doctor spoke a prayer that held more elegance than Lena would have expected, the occupants took to their meal with gusto.

"Your help here is greatly appreciated, Miss Lowrey," Annabelle said, moving a pile of purple-hull peas around on her plate.

"Happy to do it." Had she the time, she would do more. Goodness, they certainly needed it. "Besides, it's good to tend patients again."

"You've spent a long while as a nurse?"

Lena scraped a silver fork through a pile of stewed okra, revealing a delicate blue pattern on the plate underneath. "I was close to earning my degree when I got my diagnosis and had to quit."

"She claims to have a tumor inside her head."

The unexpected voice startled her, and she dropped her fork. How had she not noticed Caleb across from her? He sat rigid in his chair, his damp hair pushed behind his ears. She ventured her gaze lower. Instead of the dirty uniform from earlier, he now wore a tan shirt of coarse material with a row of small metal buttons extending from a cleanly shaven throat to the swell of a broad chest. She swallowed and whipped her gaze back to his face.

One stormy eye assessed her, then lit with a spark. His lips curved.

Lena cleared her throat. "Who would claim to have a tumor if it were not true?"

Annabelle leaned closer. "Oh, my." Her voice tightened with pity and then her eyes dawned with perceived understanding.

The look grated on Lena's nerves. "It doesn't make me crazy." She hoped.

Annabelle set down her fork and dabbed her mouth with her napkin. "Having watched you work today with skill, confidence, and keen intelligence, I would not be inclined to believe you suffer from a softening of the mind."

The reassurance should not have meant so much to her, but the way Lena's breath slipped from her lungs in a strange gush of contentment proved otherwise.

"I don't see how such a thing is possible, as there is no evidence of it," Caleb said. His tone held suspicion, but not malice.

"Believe what you will," Lena said. "Just because you cannot see the tumor doesn't mean it isn't there."

"I am not one to easily believe what I cannot see."

"Oh?" Annabelle gave Lena a small turn of her lips that almost hinted at a conspirator's smile. "Then I fear your faith must be examined, Sergeant, as I am sure you have not yet seen our Lord, but you still know of his presence."

Caleb glowered. "That's different."

"Perhaps." Annabelle took another delicate bite,

her refinement in this place of filth and chaos a mystery.

"Tell me about yourself, Ca—" Lena cut herself off, knowing the use of his first name would offend him. "Sergeant."

The din of the other soldiers filled the room, but she had no trouble hearing his deep voice over their clamor. "What do you wish to know?"

She shrugged. "The usual. Where are you from, what do you do…."

"Do? I fight for the Confederate army. My family lives on the coast."

Lena lifted the glass set next to her plate to her lips, but the overwhelming strength of the smell of raw milk had her replacing it on the table. "Why do you fight in this war?"

Suspicion clouded his eye, and he set down his fork. "To protect life and property."

"By property, of course, you mean slaves."

The din in the room quieted.

"And what makes you think I own slaves?"

Heat tingled up her spine. "You, uh, are a Southern man in eighteen sixty-four."

He eyed her as though she truly were insane. "And we are all wealthy enough for that, huh? Perhaps you have mistaken me for another. My father owns a wood shop, and my brothers and I are the only workers for his trade."

Lena opened her mouth to apologize for her mistake, but he cut her off.

"And we don't own any house slaves, either."

"Oh? Then why are you fighting to keep slavery if

you don't have any slaves?" Something in her gut
warned she'd poked a hornet's nest, but she refused to
back down.

"Miss Ross, did you know you'd brought an abolitionist into your house?" One of the soldiers broke into
their conversation, his tone too coarse for it to be a
light-hearted jab.

Annabelle folded her hands on the table in front of
her while her gaze probed Lena's face. "Are you an
abolitionist, Miss Lowrey?"

"You mean am I against slavery? Of course I am.
It's wrong."

Caleb leaned across the table, the room having
grown strangely quiet. "And what of the government
overextending its power?"

Lena tilted her head, trying to understand the
thoughts of the time. What had Momma said? She
hadn't paid enough attention. She didn't want to incite
their anger, but neither could she remain quiet. She tried
to choose her words carefully. "Yes, I think there are
times when the government seems excessive, always
poking into everything everybody does." Caleb's
shoulders began to lower, but she wasn't finished.
"However, in this case, it is correct. Slavery had to be
stopped."

Annabelle remained quiet, and if Lena were to
guess, the light in her eyes indicated she agreed. But
many of the men grumbled and sent her scalding gazes.
Not that she cared. Sensing this may have provided her
with an opportunity, Lena rose.

The men, despite their obvious dislike of her beliefs, all came to their feet.

"I, uh, just need to go to the bathroom. You can sit back down."

Annabelle seemed confused, but before anyone could say more, Lena hurried out of the room and dashed up the stairs. It was time she put an end to this crazy thing.

Sparing only a glance at the snoring soldier, Lena found the place in the doorframe and shoved the paper inside.

There! Now to get out of here.

She slipped into the bedroom she would share with Momma in the present and closed the door. She reached behind her and undid the button just above her shoulder blades and then tugged the dress over her head.

Nothing happened.

Chapter Nine

He'd craved distraction, but when trouble came in the form of a perplexing female, he realized he'd been better off in the peace of monotony. Caleb looked around the upper hall, but the lady was nowhere to be found. He flexed his fingers. Her loyalty now clear to every man below, they would surely see to it she left this place come morning. He would make it his purpose to be sure she did not find any useful information to pass to her spies before then.

A startled cry issued from the room across from him, and he reached for the door, nearly flinging it open before catching himself. He rapped his knuckles against the hearty wood. "Miss! Are you all right?"

"Go away!"

What was she doing in there? "Miss Lowrey!" Suspicion shot through reason, and he twisted the knob. "I am coming in."

"No!" Something thumped against the door. "I am not dressed."

He paused. Truth or tactic? "For what reason?"

"Just hold on a second, will you?" Even the thickness of the door could not muffle the annoyance in her voice. Caleb clasped his hands behind his back. No matter. She could not escape from the room. He could wait.

More shuffling, and then finally the door cracked open and she peeked out at him, brown hair falling over the shoulders of a more sensible dress. He took a step back. For what reason did she present herself with unbound hair? Did she think to seduce him? She would find him not so easily had. Effecting indifference as best he could, he said, "What are you doing?"

She huffed at him, as though he were the one out of sorts. "I was changing clothes."

"In the middle of the meal?"

Her cheeks turned pink, and he had to chastise himself for the thought of how fetching it made her.

"What does it matter to you?" She narrowed her gaze. "What are you doing up here anyway?"

"I came to see what you were doing."

"Why?"

Did she truly not know? "Because you are a Federalist with a half-concocted tale and a suspicious manner."

"I'm a...oh, good gravy. This is ridiculous."

"Good gravy?" Just when he'd begun to think she might not be mad after all, she said the oddest things.

Miss Lowrey rolled her eyes. "It's an expression."

"I'm not familiar with it."

"Of course you aren't." She widened the door. "Now, if you will please excuse me."

Caleb held firm. "What are you doing?"

Her eyes flashed at him, and he had the strangest desire to seek her lips and turn that fiery passion in a different direction. Caleb trampled the thought under the cadence of reason. He was marred beyond attracting any beauties, and she was…mad. A spy! A complex, intriguing, and…

"I'm trying to leave the room." She flipped her hair over her shoulder, drawing his eye to it. "What does it look like I'm doing?"

Had she shorn her locks at some point? They fell just past the crown of her shoulders. Perhaps it was the tightness of those shiny curls that drew the lengths up shorter.

He clenched his jaw. "I'll not allow you to scandalize Miss Ross."

"To…?" She paused, seeming genuinely confused. "What?"

These games were beginning to vex him. "Enough. I grow tired of this. Present yourself in a respectable manner or do not present yourself at all. Either way, I will see to it that you leave come morning."

Now she flung the door wide and squared her shoulders. "Excuse me? Who do you think you are?"

"Who am I?" He took a step closer. "A man determined not to let a spy lead to anyone else's death!"

The fire in her seemed to douse, and she softened her stance. "I'm not a spy. Lost, yes. Confused? Even more so. But I promise you. I am not a spy, nor do I wish anyone harm." She wrapped her arms around her waist, suddenly looking vulnerable. "In fact, I'm afraid my desire to help people has caused me to be stuck here."

Despite his every instinct screaming otherwise, Caleb stepped closer. Once again the sweet scent of strawberries tickled his nose, seeming to come from the tresses that cascaded down her shoulders. "How am I to believe you?"

She looked sad. "I don't know. All I can do is tell you what I know to be true. I cannot make you believe it."

Again her words slashed him like the edge of a saber. "You sound like my brother."

"I do?"

He rubbed the back of his neck. "He said something very similar right before he died. Accused one of my men. I didn't believe him." Pain clenched his stomach like a vice. "Sam said I'd asked for the truth and he'd given it. It wasn't up to him if I believed it."

She moved closer and placed a hand on his arm.

"I didn't want to believe him. Couldn't believe that one of my own men, a man whom I had fought beside, was a traitor." His voice thickened. "But it was true."

Miss Lowry squeezed his arm, her body intoxicatingly close. "I'm so sorry. That's terrible." She peered up at him, concern evident in her searching eyes. "What happened to your brother?"

The muscle in his jaw ticked, and he nearly spat the words. "He died from the wounds inflicted upon him. Moments later, the spy shot at me. The bullet meant to kill me only grazed, costing me an eye."

Her eyes widened, and inexplicably, she reached up

and placed a hand on his shoulder, her face tilted up at him in such a way that invited his lips toward hers. Did he take what she offered? Lord help him, the temptation was strong.

Caleb set his teeth and stepped back. "What do you mean to do, woman?"

"Huh?" She tilted her head, as though she had no idea what she was doing.

If he didn't know better, he would almost believe the confusion wrinkling her brow.

She sighed. "You are a very confusing man. I'm sorry to hear about your brother." She drew her lower lip through her teeth, drawing more attention to her mouth. "Though it does explain a few things."

The temptress eased even closer and offered him a smile. "I understand now why you would be concerned about spies and have problems trusting people. And I'm sure my thoughts on slavery must make you think that I am your enemy, but I promise you I am not. I simply do not think that people should be property. It goes against my religious beliefs."

She said it with such pure sincerity, without the tiniest hint of malice, that it gave him pause. "And what religious belief is that?"

"I'm a Christian."

He grunted. "So am I."

She opened her mouth, then closed it, then opened it again as though unsure what words to use. "Yet you believe in slavery?"

"The Bible is full of slaves. Paul instructs slaves to obey their masters." He repeated words oft touted among men smoking in their parlors, though truth be told, he didn't believe it. If God freed the Jews from their slavery, Caleb doubted it pleased him to see people of any kind in chains.

She frowned. "He also says there is neither slave nor free in Christ."

Caleb shifted his feet. "Either way, I do not own slaves, so it doesn't pertain to me."

"It doesn't?"

Confounding woman! "I think it best we return to meal."

"I'm not hungry."

They stood there for several moments, a stalemate in which neither seemed inclined to give ground. Finally, Caleb sighed. "Very well." He turned on his heel.

"Caleb! Wait!"

The sound of his name from her velvety voice stirred something in him best left ignored. He paused but did not turn.

"Will you let me tend your eye?"

In so doing, he would have to display belief in her fervent, if odd, reasoning that it would help him. And if he expressed belief in that, then what else would he be admitting he believed? Still, he did not want to risk infection, and if there was a small chance it would help...

"Very well. I will submit to your unorthodox ministrations." He turned to look at her. "But in the morning, you return from whence you came. Understood?"

She spread her hands. "Believe me, if it's possible,

I'll be gone in a heartbeat."

He gave a nod even as something in him yearned for the opposite.

Lena's mind fluttered as she dabbed the reddened skin around Caleb's sutures with Peggy's vinegar. She dared a glance at his good eye, and found it fixated on her face. She pretended not to notice.

Caleb shifted under her touch, drawing her eyes back to his persistent scrutiny rather than leaving her focus on the wound where it belonged. What did he think of her? He seemed to find her annoying, but then there were things that sparked in his eye that told her otherwise. Her stomach twisted, grinding what little she'd eaten under the heels of her nervousness.

The clean scent of him filled her senses. He must have washed and changed before the evening meal. Out of that uniform, she could almost forget he was a Confederate soldier. Just a good-looking man who…

She tightened her jaw. How long had she been dabbing this suture?

Alarmed, she tried to focus back on her task but found it difficult. Why was she still here? Why hadn't the dress worked? She'd even put on the drab brown dress, hoping that maybe it would just take a few moments out of the yellow dress before the time shift could take effect. She'd half expected to disappear right in front of everyone and prove herself to Caleb, but such a triumph was denied her.

Something in her heart wanted to revel in the opportunity to stay and tend patients, one in particular, but she quickly brushed that second notion aside. She wanted to be useful, and nothing else.

Caleb remained very still, but being near the tang of the strong soap he must have used to shave continued to muddle her senses. It was masculine in an appealing way, and she marveled at her heightened awareness of this man. It was crazy! Assuming this was real, she couldn't possibly be drawn to this kind of man. Could she?

"Why do you leave your hair unbound?"

The sudden question so startled her, she dropped the rag. "Huh?"

He watched her with one golden-brown eye, and she let herself take stock of his features. His strong jaw scraped clean of whiskers. A straight, sturdy nose. Everything about him was chiseled and firm. Rugged, yet somehow refined.

She swallowed again, feeling stupid. What did he just ask? Oh, right. Her hair. "I pulled it out of the bun when I changed and then I lost my hair tie." She reached up to touch it.

His shoulders seemed to relax. "So, you don't have any pins?"

Like bobby pins? "Uh, no." A thought struck her. None of those Victorian women ever seemed to wear their hair down. Was it some kind of taboo? Duh. She should have known!

"Will this do?" He offered up a small strip of cord.

"In case you misplace your tie again?"

She nearly laughed, but he seemed so genuine she could only swallow. "Um, sure. Thanks." She took the bit of coarse string and rubbed it between her fingers. How was she supposed to use that to put her hair in a bun?

"Do not worry. I shall wait while you ready yourself." He seemed relieved and glanced toward the stairs. "They should be back any moment."

Not sure why she wished to appease him, Lena rose and quickly worked the length of her hair into a braid, then tied the little string around the bottom. Then she wrapped the braid in on itself and looped it back through, tying it in a knot at the back of her head. "Better?"

He looked up at her, and the smile that lit his face made her pulse catch. What was wrong with her?

Truthfully? Very little. She felt much better here than she did at home.

Caleb rose and approached, and her heart beat faster. Though she told herself to step away as he came nearer, she found she could not. He looked down at her, standing a good four inches or so taller. Even with his missing eye, she found him unnervingly handsome.

A wayward thought struck her. What if she were to kiss him? And why not? None of this was real. And even if it was, if she was stuck here, there would be no surgery and no cure for her tumor. Why not live a little bit of life before it was her time to die?

His eye roamed her face, and then he tilted his head slightly, as though her thoughts were plastered across her face. Maybe they were. Before she could think better of it, she snaked a hand around his neck and lifted onto her toes, planting her lips on his.

Caleb startled, but didn't pull away from her. She breathed out, enjoying the rush of adrenaline. In the next breath, he wrapped his arms around her, enveloping her in his strength. His lips caressed hers, and she pressed closer.

With the desperation to cling to life, she tangled her fingers in his hair and deepened the kiss, losing herself in the warmth of him.

He groaned and then lifted his head, depriving her of the escape she'd found in his kiss. "Do you know what you do, temptress?"

"I…" What *was* she doing? She extracted herself from his arms, embarrassment overriding her recklessness. "I don't know what came over me." She looked away. "I'm sorry."

"It is I who should apologize. I should have maintained better control."

He was sorry? She'd been the one to kiss him! Lena looked at him, and the reality of her selfishness struck her. It wasn't fair to do that to him. She shouldn't start something that clearly made him feel he'd somehow taken advantage of her. She had to remember people in this time had very different relationship expectations.

Her face heated. A kiss wouldn't just be a kiss in these times. It either meant they would now have intentions of marriage or…or that she was some kind of prostitute. A loose woman. She gasped. "I'm not going to sleep with you!"

He looked shocked. "What?"

She crossed her arms. "Just because I kissed you doesn't mean I'm some kind of prostitute, you know."

He stared at her, and the fact that he said nothing seared her. That was exactly what he thought! Humiliated, she whirled around and ran for the bedroom.

Nothing had ever stirred him quite like the unexpected embrace of a mad woman. Caleb tingled. Not only in his lips where her sweetness had taken him like a sudden thunderstorm, but in his fingers, which ached to reach for her again.

She was a spy. Or mad. Probably both. Yet none of that stopped him from crossing to the door that had slammed with finality. Men ventured back up the stairs, but he ignored their shaking heads and pointed stares.

He tapped on the door.

"Go away, Caleb!"

The sound of his name, laced with both anger and angst, had him setting his jaw and placing a hand on the knob. "I will not, Miss Lowrey. We must speak."

"I don't want to."

He turned on his heel, crossed the upper hall in three strides, and snagged the chair Sergeant Wells was about to occupy.

"What's got you all riled up?" the sergeant said, reaching for the chair Caleb lifted.

"You've played enough cards for one day, don't

you think?"

The other man seemed surprised, but whatever expression marred Caleb's face must have been enough to seam his lips.

Unless Miss Lowrey climbed out of a second story window, she wouldn't be able to leave without first speaking to him. He needed to make it clear that while he'd not expected her kiss, he did not think her a trollop. He dropped the chair directly in front of the door, then settled down to wait.

Lena pulled the dress on again, and then stomped her foot when nothing happened. Impossible! She shook the yellow fabric. "What? Did you run out of time juice?" She shook it again, fighting the burning in the back of her eyes. "Couldn't do that in the present, could you? Oh, no, you had to do it now and leave me stuck in this backward, smelly…"

She was talking to herself. No wonder they thought she was crazy. But of all the bizarre things happening, Lena knew only one for certain. She wasn't crazy. She dropped to the floor, pulling her knees up.

Think, Lena.

Nothing made sense. And the *how* or *why* she ended up here made even less sense than what had just happened. She'd kissed a stranger. And she'd enjoyed it. She groaned. What was wrong with her?

Nothing here was right. Opposite in nearly every

way from how things should be. The patients were filthy. The doctor unsanitary. The food…well, the food had been fine, but if she didn't find something better to drink than raw milk, she'd die of dehydration. Though given the ordeal of visiting the outhouse, that might not be such a bad thing.

And then there was Sergeant Caleb Dockery. Built like a tower of masculinity, he was both formidable and attractive. One moment glowering at her with that steely eye and the next watching her with keen interest. Of all the things opposite of what she was used to, Caleb Dockery took the cake.

His hands were calloused. He stood when she entered a room. He treated her like something she'd never really thought about wanting to be treated like. A lady. And the way he'd kissed her…

Lena groaned and buried her face against her knees. So what if he was like a magnet pulling at her? She didn't belong here. She had to go back home to Momma. To her own time. To her surgery.

She touched her temple. When was the last time she'd had so much energy or made it through the day without a single twinge of pain? She'd worked harder today than she had since before her diagnosis, since the height of her training. Lena looked up at the plastered ceiling as though she could see through it to God. What was he doing? How utterly ridiculous was it to get a miracle by way of a time-traveling dress?

Lena blinked away useless tears gathering in her eyes and tugged off the yellow gown. The brown one Annabelle had given her was stiff, its high collar nearly making her feel choked. She buttoned the row of small wooden buttons down the front and then held out her arms. Without a bit of skin besides her neck, head, and hands showing, surely not even an eighteen-sixties man would mistake her for a woman for hire.

It seemed that even here she could not escape not being quite what she was supposed to be. Somehow, she'd once again not been enough. Of all things, now she was not *proper* enough.

Enough. Oh, how she hated that word. Story of her life. Potential, they always said, but not quite smart enough. Cute, but not really pretty. Always slipping into the background, and always almost there, but never quite making it.

No matter how hard she'd tried, her efforts simply had never been enough. *She* was never enough. And then the tumor had come and taken all of her chances away! Lena looked around the room she'd occupied in two vastly different times. Well, maybe not all of her chances were gone. Maybe she'd been given the opportunity to do something more.

Lena squared her shoulders. Enough with *enough*. She wiped troublesome dampness from her eyes. She didn't have to be anything more than who God made her to be. Maybe she wasn't enough for anyone else, but she was enough for *him*. So perhaps it was time she started feeling good enough for herself, too. Maybe she had learned what she needed here. Now she could take that back home with her…somehow.

She gathered the yellow gown in a heap and shoved it back into the wardrobe. Its powers were depleted. If she was going to find a way out of this, she would have to think. How could she get a message back to her mother? If she scrawled something across the wall, then someone would certainly paint over it in all the years between now and when Momma would see it. If she hid it, then Momma would never find it.

How then?

She paced the room until the shadows gathered too thickly for her to see, but no answer came. Finally, she sighed and turned to the door. With no electricity, she'd need a candle.

Lena opened the door only to find Caleb sitting in a chair, blocking her path. Bandage replaced, he lifted his eyebrows underneath it, singular gaze roaming down her. She must be imagining things. Surely that was not appreciation that lit his face. No. Not with her in this frumpy sack dress and her hair a mess, and…

She squared her shoulders. "Excuse me, please."

Caleb rose slowly, coming near as he did. She had to tilt her head to look up at him.

"I wish to speak to you, Miss…." He frowned. "May I call you Amberlena?"

He remembered her whole name? She shook her head. "No."

He straightened, looking all the more fearsome for the stony set to his jaw. Even so, he did not frighten her.

"Of course. Forgive me for assuming such informality."

Lena laughed, even though it made him scowl. "That's not what I meant. No one but my mother calls me Amberlena, and then only when she's upset with me. It's a mouthful, don't you think?"

He stared at her.

Lena wrapped her arms around her middle, inexplicably self-conscious. "I mean, uh, I'd prefer you called me Lena, if that's okay."

"*Okay?*"

She worked her lower lip between her teeth. "Yeah. If it's all right with you, I prefer Lena."

He took a step closer, smelling of lye soap and…and…manliness. She chastised herself. What in the world was happening to her? If she didn't suspect the tumor didn't exist in this time, she would blame it for this irrational behavior.

"Lena."

He said her name like a caress, and she shivered. Perhaps this was why they delayed calling one another by first names. Because when someone like Caleb Dockery said a woman's first name, it was enough to make her knees weaken.

Lena stood taller, just in case he noticed and could guess her thoughts. She forced a frown. "What do you want?"

Her venom didn't have the desired effect, because he only smiled.

"As I said, I wish to speak to you."

She lifted her hands. "Fine. Say whatever you need to say."

He glanced at the men watching them. "I know it is most improper, but I would greatly prefer to speak to you in private."

"Fine." She motioned to the room behind her. "You can come in."

Aghast, Caleb took a step back. "Not in there!"

Lena peered closer at him. "Where, then? There are people everywhere."

He extended a hand toward the balcony door. "Outside?"

She followed him through the men settling down on cots for the night, aware of how their eyes seemed to follow her every move. Caleb opened the door, and the warm night air settled over her like a quilt. What time was it in the present? Had Momma awoken to find her missing?

"I need to know."

Caleb's voice whispered over the hum of cicadas. Lena turned to him with a sigh.

"What?" She flung out her hands. "That I am not crazy, or a spy, or a..." What word would they use in the old days? "A harlot?"

He looked out over the balcony, careful to keep his distance from her. Even in the waning moonlight, she could see the tense set to his shoulders.

"Against all reason, I believe you are none of those things."

The words warmed more than she cared to admit, even to herself. It shouldn't matter what this man—a stranger—thought of her. Yet it did.

"Still, I must know some specifics, as you have revealed so little. Where did you come from, and what is your purpose?"

A bitter laugh bubbled from the place she tried to

keep buried. "My purpose? That's a good question. I've wondered it myself. I thought I'd found purpose in nursing, in helping people, but then in a rather cruel twist of irony ended up being a patient rather than a nurse. Whatever my purpose should have been, it is gone now."

He moved closer, and Lena gripped the balcony rail as though it would somehow help her keep a better grip on reality.

"Your nursing skills are evident, even to one such as me. The major expressed confidence in you, a compliment not easily won." He shifted his feet. "If you intend to stay, your training would prove of great use here."

Had he not said he intended to see her leave come morning? What had changed his mind? Not that she could do anything about it. "It would seem I have no option but to stay."

Caleb stiffened again and shifted away from her. Had she said something to offend him? "Not that I don't want to help, I do, but…Oh, you wouldn't understand."

"I'd like to."

"I'm worried about Momma." Her voice hitched. "She won't know what's happened to me."

His hand settled on her shoulder, a warm weight of comfort that shouldn't stir her as it did. "And you cannot get back to her?"

"Looks like the dress ran out of power." Now she really did sound crazy. She hurried her words. "I know how that sounds, and I know you have no cause to believe me, but I found that yellow dress and when I put it on, it took me back in time." She strained to see him in the light. "To your time. When I took it off, it sent me back to my time, more than a century and a half after the end of the Civil War. But now…" She shrugged. "As you can see, I've changed clothes, but I'm still here."

He stood there for several moments until she thought the silence would be unbearable. Finally, he sighed, his breath stirring her hair. "So you have been going back and forth in time?" His voice softened as though he were speaking to a child. "Yet you have not left since you arrived."

"It seems that way, but…" She shook her head and stepped away from him. No point in explaining anything. He would never believe her. She wouldn't believe her either if she wasn't currently living the insanity. "Oh, never mind. This is pointless."

Lena stepped around him and reached for the door. "But just so you know, I have been nothing but honest with you. Even if the truth seems ridiculous, it is still the truth."

The shadows shifted, and he moved toward her, but she was already slipping into the house, wiping at tears that had no more business being on her cheeks than she had being in this time.

The next afternoon, Caleb hefted an axe over his

shoulder, glad to be out of the house and about something useful. He'd spent the night far too awake. Why must his thoughts ever return to a young woman who did not seem to make any sense?

He swatted a mosquito and looked for the wayward sapling Peggy indicated as the one meant for her cook fires. Would Lena be with her now, helping in the kitchen?

As though his thoughts summoned her to his side, Lena stepped out onto the rear porch, her slim hand shielding her eyes. The sight of her struck him, and he paused. Regardless of from whence she came, she was a vision. She wore her silky hair piled on her head, wayward curls escaping to caress cheeks slightly flushed from the heat.

Her gaze found his, and she smiled, revealing perfect white teeth. "There you are. Peggy said you were about to do some woodcutting." Her gaze roamed over him, and he wondered if she found him appealing with his suspenders hanging at his sides and his shirtsleeves rolled to his elbows.

"I am. I have been gaining sureness in compensating for my lost eye. Such tasks are beneficial for me to practice precision." He twirled the axe, unable to ignore the thrill he felt whenever she drew close.

Her smile brightened, and his nearing departure suddenly seemed undesirable. If he were to ask, would she wait for him? He thrust the thought away. What was he thinking?

"I've come to ask you a favor," she said, blessedly plucking him from his ludicrous thoughts.

Before he could think better of it, a single word rushed from his lips with far too much excitement. "Anything."

The light that brightened her eyes was worth the chink in the armor he had pointlessly tried to don against her. Her tender care and earnest sincerity ever drew him.

"I wonder if I may ask you to chop a different tree."

An odd request, but then, why should he expect anything different? "Ever do you keep me on the brink of curiosity, Miss Lowrey."

He said it with teasing, and she tossed her head like a prancing filly. He nearly laughed, a fitting picture, indeed.

"I have been told men like a challenge. Maybe it will keep you interested." She said it with a laugh, but then her eyes flew wide as though she'd revealed more than intended.

"Do you endeavor to keep my interest, Lena?" he asked, growing serious.

"I...um..." she looked behind her, then squared her shoulders and tried to speak more like a proper lady. "Come, I shall show you the other tree."

His question answered by her pink cheeks and stuttering avoidance of her statement, Caleb grinned. "Worry not. It takes bafflingly little effort on your part for you to hold my attention."

She arched warm brown eyebrows. "Bafflingly?"

"Indeed. You always seem to do something unexpected, though you continue to prove your knowledge and aptitude." Suddenly too self-aware, he averted his gaze from her questioning features. "You keep the attention of all here with your unconventional ways."

Her shoulders drooped slightly, and he berated himself. "Though I daresay you tend to hold my eye more than any others'."

Moment gone, she walked toward the side of the house, moving gracefully in a borrowed cotton dress. "The tree I want is over here."

They rounded the house, and Caleb hesitated. "That one is much larger than the one Peggy indicated." He tilted his head back. "Its growth will provide shade for the side of the house."

Lena pressed her lips together. "I know. But it must be this one."

"Why?"

"When we come here in the future, this is a massive, ancient oak. I'm thinking if I have you cut it now, it will never grow into the giant shade tree we parked beneath. If it suddenly disappears, then maybe Momma will believe me." Pain flooded her eyes. "I have some other plans, too, but..." She looked away. "I'm just hoping that in some way I can get word back to her about what happened to me."

She appeared so hopeless that even if it were pure madness, Caleb wanted nothing more than to give her comfort in whatever way he could. "Very well. Though you know Peggy will not be pleased."

Lena drew near, placing a hand on his sleeve. "You cannot know the depth of my gratitude. Thank you." Her eyes glistened. "Thank you for believing me."

He wanted to tell her he didn't believe a word of it. That he did it only because which tree was cut meant nothing to him, and he only wanted to keep her from being upset. But with each pound of his axe, he proved himself wrong. If he truly thought her mad, why did he find himself believing her? Trusting her? Wanting nothing more than to protect her when he should distance himself as far as possible?

Chapter Ten

$\mathcal{C}$ aleb readied himself for bed with a smile that could not be torn from his lips.

"It's good to see you in such high spirits," Private Jenkins said as Caleb settled on his cot in the dim light.

He hadn't been aware anyone else remained awake. He'd spent too long with Lena out of doors this evening, pushing far past the confines of propriety but finding he didn't care.

"Thanks, Paul," he said, eschewing titles for a man who'd become more friend than soldier under his command.

The man chuckled as he fluffed his pillow. "That is the way of it. The right woman can do things to a man he never thought possible."

Paul's words, laced with longing and sadness, tugged at him. Even after his friend's breathing turned to snores, Caleb contemplated what Paul had said.

Everything he had ever known had been flung into chaos because of one confusing woman. Caleb tossed onto his back, Private Pearson's rumbling snores more annoying than usual. Moonlight slipped through the windows and glided across the floor, caressing the door that hid the young nurse who'd stolen more from him than just his attention.

Moments with her passed far too quickly, and though he had first watched her with the intent of catching her as a spy, he soon gave up such a notion. Lena seemed to have no interest in anything other than throwing every bit of her energy into caring for the men here. She had tended them with as much skill—nay, more—than the doctor. Already, five of his brothers in arms were ready to return to the nearby encampment in direct response to her treatment for their fevers.

The thought made him shift again. Yesterday morning's visit from Major Evers confirmed what he had tried to ignore. He would return to duty soon. Though he still remained blind in one eye, he felt sure his reflexes would keep him alive.

He hoped.

He had yearned to return to duty ever since a jostling wagon had first deposited him at Rosswood. He'd seethed for days in a medical tent before being sent here to wallow in the humiliation of having his eye taken from him. He'd longed to return to usefulness, to throw himself into anything that could help him forget what happened to his brother.

He probed at the new patch Miss Ross had sewn to replace his bandage. The skin underneath no longer itched and burned, no doubt due in part to Lena and her radical treatments. Too many of the men who had long suffered here were finding swift recovery under her hand for it to be coincidence.

Rather than spying, it must have been the hand of Providence that sent her here. But why? The cicadas swelled, taunting him with questions he could not answer. How could he believe her tale? It was utter madness. She'd nearly begged him to cut a tree in the vain hope she'd reach her mother. Caleb had sensed vast sadness in her and had often wondered if she'd made up the fanciful tale to cover a pain she could not escape. But today, he'd realized that she seemed sad because of the tale itself. And that twisted his insides into a knot.

Caleb stared at the ceiling and forced himself to examine things he'd tried to ignore. Perhaps, like his brother, she spoke a truth he could not fathom, which led him to imagine his own explanations. Regardless, he was almost loath to return to duty. There could be only one explanation for such a shift in his thinking. He could not bear to leave the peculiar Miss Amberlena Lowrey.

Lena sat on the front steps of the house, staring up at the stars. They were bright here with no artificial lights to drown them out. The sky seemed a massive swath of ebony silk coated in diamonds.

By now, Momma must be a complete wreck. Lena wrapped her arms around her knees. In some ways, these had been the longest days of her life, and in other ways, the shortest. She'd thrown everything she had into tending the patients. She was useful again, and it felt good. Part of her nagged that saving men who may have been meant to die would alter the course of history, but she'd come to be at peace with it. If God somehow wanted her to be here, then nothing she did would alter his plans.

But, oh, Lord, what about Momma? How long will you need me to help here and leave her to worry?

The stars glittered, but she received no revelation from them. Her thoughts shifted from one of the two great things that occupied her mind to the other. She *needed* to go home...but in a way she couldn't explain, she wanted to stay. This place was hectic and all the customs foreign, but oddly, she felt comfortable here. At peace, and, inexplicably, almost as if she belonged. Weird and impossible, yes, but no less impossible than being here in the first place. She felt healthy and robust, even more so than she had before she'd developed the tumor. The simplicity and slower pace of life, even in a busy hospital, seemed to meld with an inner rhythm she hadn't even known she possessed.

And then there was Caleb. Could it be him, more than anything else, that kept her awake tonight? Was it the stirring of her heart that gave her the ridiculous longing to stay here and see what could become of it?

She should be sleeping, but these quiet moments outside in the cooler air were slivers of solitude, moments when responsibilities slumbered and her patients rested in the comfort of good care. She'd check them once more before returning to the room she'd crept out of, but for a few minutes longer, she would allow herself this comfort.

Lena pulled the dress and its heavy underskirts up over her knees and extended her legs and bare feet down the steps, leaning back. What she wouldn't give for a pool. Mississippi in the humid days of September was bad enough, but with no air-conditioning or even the ability to wear shorts, it was stifling.

Sweat dampened her scalp and slid down her cheek. She needed a shower and proper deodorant, but no one here seemed to notice. Last night Annabelle had given her water with Peggy's fragrant herbs and some flower petals to give herself a sponge bath with, so that was something at least. It didn't last, though, with the abundance of layers one had to wear in all this heat.

She pushed the sleeves up as far as the tight buttons would allow and then finally decided to just take off the dress and two petticoats. Underneath, she wore what Annabelle called a chemise, which was really just a long nightgown. Given the fact Peggy had also given her a pair of bloomers, which were really like full-length lacy pants, she was more covered in just those things than if she'd been wearing shorts and a tee back home. She'd gone through quite a bit of arguing with Peggy, but in the end, had still found herself dressed in the entire roasting ensemble this morning.

First, she'd been made to wear the pantaloons, then the chemise, then the corset…which had given Lena pause until she realized it wasn't something out of a lingerie catalog but rather a functional item to help keep the ties of all those petticoats from digging into her waist. She had two of them to wear under her dress, and had figured out that was the minimum. If she were doing anything other than nursing, Peggy had said, she would likely be wearing a set of hoops, which would then be covered with more petticoats, before she could put on a skirt and bodice. The very thought brought beads of sweat to her brow. If it hadn't made the two women decidedly more comfortable in her presence, she would have refused.

No wonder women had given up on such complicated fashions. Working in scrubs was much easier. Lena unhooked the corset and tossed it on her dress, then leaned back to enjoy the cool moonlight in the long nightgown. Still modestly covered from collarbone to ankles, but tremendously cooler.

She lay back on the wood of the porch and closed her eyes, content to listen to the cicadas and the croak of frogs.

Peaceful.

A sound, one that didn't belong in the quiet of the night in a time where no cars or commercial jets existed, perked her ears. Lena sat up.

It came again—a crunching sound. Was someone wandering around the house? Her experience with the dangers of the Civil War had thus far been limited to the rigors of nursing, but she wasn't entirely ignorant of history. Roving bands of soldiers, lawless bandits, and desperate citizens could all prove perilous to a woman out alone in the night.

Lena scooped up her clothing and quietly crossed the porch. She needed to get to bed anyway.

Something scraped. It sounded like…

Lena turned. Before she could react, someone grabbed her in a crushing embrace, sending her pulse galloping. She twisted and tried to use the man's weight against him as she had been taught in self-defense class, but she found it entirely useless.

"Shhh…I only come to take what you've been offering."

The voice made her skin crawl. Lena struggled anew, her efforts thwarted by the man's strength and her own panic.

"Come, let's go somewhere more private."

Lena screamed.

Caleb jarred from the light sleep to which he had finally succumbed. What was that? He swung out of his cot, and instinctively rushed to Lena's door. He rapped lightly.

"Lena? Are you all right?"

No response. The hairs on the back of his neck stood on end. No one else in the house stirred. Had it been a dream that had awakened him? For some reason, his instincts told him otherwise. Deciding it would be better to know, he pushed the door open.

Moonlight marched across the floor but did not give enough illumination for him to see into the chamber without breaching the threshold. Praying she would forgive his impertinence, he whispered her name again and then stepped inside the room.

Dodging shadows, he eased closer to the bed, hoping to find her sleeping and then leave as quietly as he'd entered without her any wiser. Measuring his stride, he finally came to stand next to the canopy bed.

Only to find it empty.

Alarm spiking, he retreated back through the room, leaving the door open behind him. Should anyone else awaken, they would discover her chamber vacant.

A wayward thought, one he'd thought he had overcome, peppered his senses. Did she conduct spy activity during the night?

Caleb moved around the sleeping men in the hall. He would check downstairs and see if she was moving about in secret. The stairs groaned twice upon his descent, as though to warn those on the lower level of his approach. The front hall no longer contained patients, and only one parlor still functioned as a hospital space. He avoided the library, as Miss Ross had rightfully reclaimed its use, and checked the men in the parlor next to the dining room.

They slept peacefully, the quiet in the house an affront to his chafed nerves. Perhaps it had only been a dream. Another frightful reliving of that day he'd lost Sam. Caleb turned back toward the foyer, trying to convince himself all was as it should be. But never before had that dream startled him awake without the first recollection of its horror.

Even if a dream were to blame for his wakefulness, the fact remained that Lena was not in her chamber. He stepped through the foyer, careful not to trip on the various medical items and crates clustered about.

Something scraped, and a muffled noise pierced the front door. Caleb stilled, his hand instinctively going for the weapon that no longer hung at his side. Regardless, he quickened his pace, laying a hand on the cool metal doorknob.

Keeping his back to the frame, he cracked open the door and willed his vision to split the murky shadows. The sound came again, farther away this time, as though someone dragged a flour sack down the walk.

Miss Ross had little enough as it was. He would not let some miscreant make off with a single thing. Caleb flung open the door and stalked out into the night, only to be greeted by a sight that turned his blood cold.

Chapter Eleven

aleb blinked in the dim light, but the sight before him didn't change. Lena, completely indecent, stood wrapped in another man's arms. His blood boiled, the cold of shock instantly melting under the fire churning in his chest. She struggled, trying to do one of those strange arm flailing things she did when he had grabbed her without invitation. Realization set in, and he lurched forward.

"Caleb!"

"Hold it right there, Dockery." That voice, holding the same contempt it had over many a hand of cards, spiked in the humid air. "I got her first. You can have your turn after."

"Wells! What are you doing?" Caleb moved closer.

Sergeant Wells hauled Lena closer to him, coming up against a cluster of thorny rosebushes surrounding an angel statue.

"I command you to unhand that lady at once."

Sergeant Wells snorted. "You don't outrank me. You and I both know this here ain't no lady, and I'm not giving up my go at her. You want to take that up with the Major, you go ahead."

Lena whimpered, and the vulnerable sound coming from one so strong set his teeth on edge. "Please, Caleb, I don't—"

Wells cut off her words. "Quiet, harlot."

"She's not a trollop!" Caleb stepped closer, his fists balling. "You have seen her work as a nurse. This is utter madness." He took another step, his socked feet hot on the brick walkway. "Now unhand her."

Sergeant Wells laughed. "You have seen her flaunting! Raising her skirts, teasing with bits of skin. I'm finally coming to take what she's been offering." He put his face in her tumbled hair, breathing in, and then looked back at Caleb with a grin. "Aye, this vixen has been teasing. Can't blame a man for finally giving in to the temptation she offers."

"I didn't offer you anything, you filthy jerk!" She struggled against the broad expanse of Sergeant Wells's chest, but could not free herself.

Caleb had seen enough. In one stride, he had hold of Wells's shoulder. In another breath, his hand snaked up the side of the man's neck and found a hold in the fleshy area beneath Wells's chin.

The sergeant lost his grip on Lena, and she bolted free, shooting insults at him even as she scurried back toward the porch. Wells shifted and, before Caleb could react, smashed his jaw with a fist.

Caleb reeled back. Curse the missing eye that blinded his left side!

"Now look what you've done!" Wells's eyes darted

to where Lena had bounded away. "I had her going with me until you showed up."

Caleb rubbed his jaw, stepping back to keep Wells in sight.

"Think what you want, Dockery, but that little trollop was already stripped down when I found her." The words snaked across Caleb's nerves. "And she *was* going with me to the privacy of the woods."

Caleb lunged and swung at the same moment, thrusting his full weight into the forward explosion of his fist. It landed with a satisfying crack, splintering Wells's nose.

He cursed, stumbling back into the roses and tripping. "You've broken my nose!"

"Good thing there's a doctor nearby." Caleb smirked, rubbing his hand. "Best you get in there and explain how you managed to get injured in the middle of the night."

He stalked back toward the house only to find Lena still standing on the porch in her underdress, clothing clutched to her chest. Her eyes were wide in the moonlight, filled with anger rather than humiliation. What had caused her to be in such a state out of doors? Would he never understand this woman?

Coming to a stop at the bottom of the stairs, he could not contain the bark of his words. "Shouldn't you be covering yourself?"

She blinked at him, and then looked down at her flimsy attire. "Seriously? I'm wearing long pants *and* a full-length dress!"

He stared at her, trying to reason the look of frustration on her face. She looked past him to where Wells still sat on the ground holding his nose and cursing.

"Look," she said, "I know you don't get it, but I am not used to wearing all these layers in the heat with no air-conditioning. I was out here alone, and I just wanted to cool off." She glared at him. "I did nothing to lead that man to think I wanted..." She shook her head.

Caleb flexed his fingers. Again she spoke strange words as though she were from a different land. Or perhaps time? "And you don't think lifting your skirts and showing men your ankles leads them to think otherwise?"

"Oh, good gravy." She crossed her arms, bunching the fabric thankfully covering her bosom. "When it's ninety degrees, we wear shorts and tank tops." She put the side of her hand to the top of her thigh. "Shorts are pants that stop here."

He gawked at her. She expected him to believe women walked around with their entire leg showing to strangers?

"And I won't even tell you what a bikini is. You'd probably faint."

"You think me effeminate, that I would faint like a woman?"

She had the audacity to roll her eyes toward the porch ceiling. "You're being ridiculous."

Before he could convince himself to do otherwise, he took the steps and clasped her elbow, trying not to notice how little fabric separated her skin from his touch. "Inside, before everyone else sees you in such a state of indecency."

She made no move to escape him, only stood looking up at him with luminous eyes that seemed to hold genuine confusion. For all the peculiar words she spoke, one thing he believed true in the days he'd spent with her—this woman did not lie. Whatever foolishness she spouted, she seemed to wholeheartedly believe.

He tried to nudge her forward again, not wishing to physically haul her away as Wells had done. Somehow, he sensed that in so doing, he would lose the respect he had on more than one occasion glimpsed in her eyes when she looked upon him. "No matter what you believe, can you not see that the men here do not believe likewise? They are not accustomed to seeing any part of a woman's leg unless…" He cleared his throat. "Unless he knows her."

"He knows her? What does *that* mean? Every person in this house knows me."

Sergeant Wells gained his feet and started making his way toward the porch. Caleb had no doubt he would cause a fuss once inside, and he did not want the household to see Lena in such a state.

Caleb gestured toward the house. "Please, go inside, Lena."

She glanced back at Wells. "Oh." She narrowed her eyes, then they suddenly rounded with understanding. "How stupid of me. You mean to say that a man doesn't see a woman's legs unless he's sleeping with her."

Heat crept up his ears. "Or, in the case outside of marriage, he isn't sleeping at her side, but rather—"

She held up a hand. "I get it."

Thank heavens. He didn't want to have to explain it to her.

Lena slipped inside, bounding up the stairs with such speed and grace that she once again reminded him of a fleeing doe. He stepped into the front hall, baffled by her. She knew things a proper lady shouldn't. She showed no humiliation at being seen in only her nightdress. Yet Caleb simply could not believe this woman a harlot, even though all the evidence suggested otherwise.

So, then, what did he believe?

The front door slammed, reverberating through the house. Caleb turned, waiting for the commotion that would ensue. As suspected, there were startled yelps throughout the lower floor. Fool man. He would get someone shot.

Sergeant Wells sneered at Caleb through the blood covering his mouth. Even in the dim light of the full moon beyond the windows, it glimmered like spilled ink. "Let it be known that Sergeant Dockery has struck his fellow soldier!"

Caleb set his shoulders. And here he'd thought Lena the one with a propensity for the dramatic. They stared at each other until Major Thrasher tromped down the stairs, dressed only in rumpled trousers and a partially buttoned shirt.

"What is going on here?" The major looked at Caleb and Wells in turn, and then around at the others who had gathered.

What would happen when all these men returned to duty and the army moved on? Where would Lena go when she was no longer the nurse here?

"Are you not going to answer me, Sergeant?"

Caleb saluted Major Thrasher. "He speaks truth, sir. I did strike him."

Major Thrasher stroked his bewhiskered chin and looked back at Wells, who seemed to have thought Caleb would deny it, given the way his jaw slackened.

The major looked back at Caleb. "And your reason?"

"It was the only way I saw to bring an end to the situation."

Major Thrasher scowled. "It is the middle of the night. You will speak plain, and in full, about the *situation!*"

Caleb glanced toward the stairs, then back at Wells, who now looked infuriatingly smug. "I caught Sergeant Wells in the act of attempting to dishonor a lady."

Major Thrasher swung his gaze to Wells. "Is this true?"

Sergeant Wells snorted, then grimaced and touched his broken nose. "He wanted to go first with the harlot and when I said no, he took a swing at me."

By now another handful of men had gathered to watch. Caleb avoided looking at them. "That is not the case, sir. There are no painted women here, as you know."

The officer looked between the two men. "I take it you refer to Miss Lowrey?"

Wells looked smug again. "Yes, sir. I only meant to take what she offered. She removed her garments herself. I did not take them from her, as he implies."

"Is this true, Sergeant Dockery?"

Caleb clasped his hands behind his back. "The lady was sitting in private, alone, trying to cool herself after a long day of aiding the wounded. Sergeant Wells came upon her and, rather than turning himself away, sought to haul her against her will from the house and out to the lawn."

Major Thrasher reddened and focused on the other man. "What say you, Sergeant Wells?"

He stood at attention. "She is a harlot, sir." He thrust his chin toward Caleb. "And he only wants her for himself. You've seen the way he looks at her."

"Enough!" Major Thrasher yelled. "I will deal with this in the morning. Find your beds."

"But, sir, what about my nose?"

"Best you wash it before you find your cot." Major Thrasher turned toward the stairs, giving Caleb a slight nod before he ascended to the bedchamber Miss Ross had afforded him.

Thankfully, Sergeant Wells took his rest in the lower floors and, better still, was to return to his regiment at the end of the week. As Caleb was in Company J and Wells served in Company B, Caleb wouldn't have to suffer his presence much longer.

He took the stairs with heavy steps, thankful to see Lena's door firmly closed and the men returning to their beds. But how many of them thought the same of her as Wells? Would others attempt what he had?

Caleb clenched his teeth. How would he protect her once he returned to duty?

Chapter Twelve

 $\mathcal{W}$ hy could she not escape? Lena pulled the yellow gown over her head, said a prayer, and then pulled it off again.

Nothing!

Fighting tears that burned the back of her throat and stung her eyes, she dropped to the floor and wrapped her arms around her knees. Why could she not get back to Momma?

A knock came at the door. "Miss Lowrey, may I speak with you?"

Annabelle. Great. How could she explain what had happened? Sighing, Lena rose, pulled on the yellow gown again, and then cracked open the door.

With clasped hands, Annabelle offered a sweet smile that held only compassion. Lena lowered her eyes and pulled the door open wide enough for Annabelle to enter.

The teen stood there a moment, looking far too composed.

The silence stretched until Lena could no longer

stand it. "No matter what they say, I did *not* invite that man to grab me!"

Annabelle nodded, and then in a swift movement grasped Lena's hand. "Miss Lowrey, you must listen to me."

"Lena."

She inclined her head, golden curls sweeping her shoulder. Again Lena was struck by how young, and at the same time wise, the girl looked.

"Lena, I have begun to fear for your safety."

"Yeah, I have that problem myself." She tried for a smirk, but it fell flat.

Annabelle gave Lena's hand another squeeze, the thick shadows nearly making her features unreadable. "It is more than the wayward soldiers, I'm afraid."

Lena frowned. What could be worse than that?

"My grandfather... Well, he isn't really my grandfather, but..." She dropped Lena's hand and turned away. "Never mind. It is not your concern. However, as his sickness worsens, so does his temper."

It was not at all what Lena had expected her to say. Yesterday, a wizened old man with hawkish features had arrived in a cloud of resentment and snarled words, but since then had remained locked in his room on the bottom floor. She'd glimpsed him only one other time, on his way out to what they called *the necessary* in the rear yard. Only Annabelle entered his domain to bring meals. He wouldn't even let Peggy do it.

"Why?" The old fellow's moods hardly seemed of any consequence when there were brutes driven to violence by the mere sight of an exposed calf. If she weren't so upset, she would laugh. Imagine what would happen to those men if they got sent to *her* time!

"…and that's why it is better to stay out of his way. If he gets it in his head to see you removed from here, there will be nothing I can do to stop it."

Lena focused on Annabelle again. "You could say something. All you have to do is tell him no."

She remained silent for a few breaths, and Lena leaned closer to try to see her better in the murky light.

Finally, Annabelle's quiet words filled the room. "You truly don't understand our ways here, do you?"

"I'm afraid not."

"Is it that much different up north? My mother has family there, and I've often wondered about them. Especially since the start of the war…"

Something in her tone piqued Lena's curiosity. "Tell me, do you side with North or South?"

Another prolonged silence. She fiddled with her hands. "My father fought for the Confederacy."

"I didn't ask that. I asked what *you* believe."

"Peggy is the closest to a mother I've had since I was very young." Her voice seemed to gain strength, and a fire Lena had not yet heard from her leapt into Annabelle's words. "If I had my way, not she nor anyone else would be owned like one owns a horse."

Lena had thought as much. But how much trouble would a lone Southern woman get herself into harboring such thoughts in this time? "Good thing this war is almost over. What is this? September?" She counted on her fingers and answered her own question. "By spring it will all be over."

Annabelle huffed. "People have been saying that for years. I grow weary of it."

"Yes, but—"

Another knock at the door. "Lena?"

Annabelle put a hand on her hip, and though Lena could not distinguish her face in the gloom, she sensed Annabelle's eyes held questions.

"I am talking to Ann...uh...Miss Ross at the moment, Sergeant Dockery. Perhaps we could speak tomorrow?" Really? Where had that come from? Geez, she was starting to talk like these people now.

There were some shuffling noises, and then a pause. "If it would not overly tire you, I would prefer this matter not wait."

Annabelle opened the door, spilling slivers of silver moonlight in from the hall. It pooled around Caleb's shoulders but kept his face in shadows.

"Sergeant. What urgent matter do you need to discuss with a lady at this hour?"

The rise of his chin indicated he was looking over Annabelle's head to Lena. "Only this. I am deeply sorry for the fright Sergeant Wells gave you this evening." His voice hardened. "However, I would strongly suggest that in the future, you refrain from making yourself appear willing if you indeed are not."

Heat coursed through her stomach. "Excuse me? Are you saying this is *my* fault?"

"Miss Lowrey is not from here." Annabelle's words sounded oddly apologetic. "Perhaps they do things much differently up north."

"You don't need to make excuses for me." Lena

crossed her arms over her pounding heart. "I am not from the north. But none of that even matters. You people will believe only what you want to. I am not a spy. I am not a prostitute." Despite her best efforts, her voice trembled. "I am not even supposed to be here!"

"Then why are you?"

Caleb's words, spoken softly yet with an icy edge, sliced right through her anger to the true emotion underneath. Lena sucked a breath as a realization slammed into her like a freight train. She put her hand to her chest and stepped back, bumping up against the bed.

Stupid. How could she have been so stupid? She'd let herself get caught up in this madness. She'd somehow, inexplicably, developed feelings for a rugged, fierce man she barely knew. Despite all logic, all reason, she cared for him—a virtual stranger. And because of that, his tone cut her in ways she'd thought herself hardened to.

Since the cruelty of children throughout her elementary years, Lena had learned not to take stock in the words of others. Momma taught her to be herself, no matter what. Over the years, that had become letting people in less. The less they knew, the less they could harm her.

It had worked for years. But somehow, in this strange place, she had let herself forget all of those things. She'd opened herself to this time, to the work here, and worst of all, to him.

And now, the words he flung flayed her heart. At least it was too dark for him to see the tears stinging her eyes.

"I…" She what? What could she say? She couldn't tell him the rejection clinging to his words cut deep into a heart that should not beat in cadence to the very thought of him. She should not wish, even now under his scrutiny and suspicion, to reach for him and feel the touch of his lips again.

"Lena?" Annabelle moved closer, worry in her tone. "Are you unwell?"

She put a hand to her head. "No. I just need…" Where were her words?

"I am going to get Peggy." In a sweep of rustling fabric, Annabelle scurried past Caleb and out into the hall, leaving her alone with a man she should be afraid of but wasn't.

He hovered in the doorway, as though he knew his very presence unnerved her.

"Go away, Caleb. You don't understand."

"You are right. I don't." He stepped over the threshold. "I don't understand why you wish to flaunt yourself, even when you know it invites men's eyes."

"I did not mean to invite anyone's eyes." Well, perhaps only one eye… Good gravy! What was wrong with her? She averted her gaze. "I need to get out of here."

"Yes." Relief flooded his tone. "I think that would be for the best."

Another twist of the knife to her gut. "You want me to go?" She clenched her teeth. Had she really just sounded that pathetic?

He took another step into the room, his words

slow and measured. "They have recalled me to my unit. I will leave the next time my commander returns. I think it wise that you not stay here."

"You're leaving so soon?" She narrowed her eyes. "I'm not convinced you are fully healed enough to do so."

Another step and he was close enough that if she were to reach out, she could touch him. But she wouldn't.

"It is my duty. If I can march and shoot, then I am to return to duty."

Mouth dry, she sagged against the bed. Why did it matter so much to her? She didn't belong here and his life would be what it had always been. A life he had already lived without her. "But what if you have trouble seeing? Couldn't that get you…"

"Killed? I suppose." He watched her closely, as though he could sense the turmoil she needed to hide.

Lena bit back her words. He was a soldier. He would go back to do what fighting men did. She clutched the gown at her chest. Then she would be here alone. She blinked away tears that threatened to expose the emotions swarming inside her.

He reached out to take her hand, but she pulled away. "Please understand. I must return to my men." He dropped his arm back to his side. "But I do not wish to leave here knowing you may come to harm." He shifted his stance. "I could not bear to know you might be in any danger."

So he cared? She invited further rejection in the darkness even though her senses were screaming for her not to. "Why do you care what happens to me?"

He stiffened. "I think you already know the answer to that. Or have you so soon forgotten we've shared something intimate?"

"Intimate? We haven't—" Her face heated. "Oh, you mean the kiss." The fact that he considered their kiss intimate implied something treasured and not merely a casual occurrence.

Still, she needed to hear him say something. She needed to know for sure. Lena slowly allowed her gaze to settle on his face. "Don't you see? I've tried, but I can't go home. If you leave, I'll be stuck here. Alone." There. She'd said it. Opened herself to his scorn.

"You will not be alone." His words were soft, a caress that reached across the shadows separating them. "You have Miss Ross. She is a kind and compassionate woman. She will make sure you are not destitute until you find your way to somewhere safer. Perhaps with family?"

Lena nodded. Rejected. Why would she think being in another time would change that? "Of course."

He lifted his arm as though to reach for her again, but then rubbed the back of his neck instead. "Promise me you will not go about in your underpinnings again."

Fighting irrational tears, Lena steeled her voice. "What does it matter to you? You've made it clear you have no cares for me beyond the notion that I am a disgrace and a distraction to your soldiers."

"They are not my soldiers. And that is not—"

"Go away, Sergeant Dockery. I don't wish to suffer your company another moment."

He took a step back. "Lena…" He ground out her name, almost like a groan, and her heart wrenched.

She pushed off the bed. "Did you not hear me? I said go away. Leave me alone!"

He spun on his heel and stalked through the door. Holding back a sob, she slammed it behind him, not caring who she woke up in the process.

Lena grabbed the dress and pulled it off, throwing it in a heap on the floor. Left in her *underpinnings*, she climbed into the large canopy bed and flung the covers over her head.

"Please, God," she whispered to the ceiling. "Please, just let me go home."

Life had seemed less complicated in the heat of battle than it did now that Lena Lowrey had appeared in his life. Caleb stared at her door, jaw clenched so tightly it ached. She had been right. Why *did* he care so much what she did? She was not his responsibility. He had not been the one to bring her to a strange house and leave her without aid or chaperone.

Except, she had not come through the front door. He rubbed his chin, considering. In fact, she hadn't even come up the stairs the day she had arrived. He knew, because he'd been playing cards in the hall all morning. She had appeared out of the bedroom.

Impossible. Could she really have been telling the truth? It didn't make any sense. None, except it explained the strange phrases she spoke, her lack of understanding of customs and, above all else, her insistence. Honesty had shown from her eyes, yet he had ignored it. And what sane man wouldn't? She claimed something entirely unthinkable.

But...perhaps true? He pinched the bridge of his nose. He would have to make a decision. He must either trust her without any proof and make his intentions known, or he must forget her and go back to his life in the army.

The answer seemed obvious. She was a madwoman, and he needed to forget her. Why, then, did he feel sickened by the thought? What was it about this woman, this mad, beautiful being who had captured him so? She was nothing like any woman he had ever met. And perhaps that was why she had captivated him in a way no woman ever had. Even with his grotesque deformity, he has seen the spark of attraction in her eyes, and—dare he hope?—something more.

So, what was he going to do about it?

Miss Ross came up the steps, Peggy in tow. "I think she sleeps, Miss Ross. There has been no movement from her room."

Peggy's grumble came from behind Miss Ross. "Dat figures. After I done had to get myself up."

"I still think we should check on her, Peggy. Just to be sure."

Peggy's voice softened at Miss Ross's concern. "All right, Miss Belle. If you think it be for the best."

The women moved on to the room, knocking softly. Despite his better judgment, Caleb stepped closer.

"You got it bad, don't you, Sergeant?"

Caleb stopped. He'd forgotten all about the other man who occupied the hall with him. "I thought you were asleep, Jenkins."

The man yawned. "Was, sir. But sure is hard for a man to sleep with all this commotion going on around here."

No response came from the room. Miss Ross knocked again.

"Life is sure short," Jenkins said, his tone serious and holding none of the usual mirth Caleb had become accustomed to hearing. "Shorter, I think, and more uncertain during war."

"And?" He chided himself for his gruffness even as the single bit-off word leapt from his tongue.

Jenkins seemed to take no offense. He rolled up off his cot and ran a hand through shaggy brown hair. Caleb could barely see him in the dim light, but knew his features well. At this moment, his eyes likely held compassion. He had a way of bringing calm to any situation and could often see what men thought even if they didn't say it.

Which unnerved Caleb at the moment.

"And, since life is so uncertain, it might be best that you declare your feelings for the lady while you still can."

Peggy knocked this time, shaking the door. If anyone in this house had been sleeping, they no longer had the luxury.

"Private Jenkins?" Caleb clenched his fists, warring emotions dousing over him like scalding oil.

"Yes, sir?"

"Keep yourself to your own affairs."

The man lay back on his cot. "Yes, sir."

"Miss Lowrey?" Peggy pounded again. "We comin' in!"

Caleb stepped closer and stood at the hem of Miss Ross's dressing gown. Surely Lena could not have slept through that. Why had she not opened the door?

"If you plan on making yourself known, sir, now would be a good time," Jenkins said, disregarding direct orders to keep to himself.

Ignoring the infuriatingly insightful soldier, Caleb moved to fill the open door frame behind the women. Peggy stood with her hands on her hips, her figure blocking the shadowed bed.

The hairs on the back of his neck tingled. "Is she unwell?"

Miss Ross stepped around Peggy and peered up at him. "Why didn't you say you saw her leave? Why tell me she was sleeping?"

"What? What are you talking about?" He moved past her to the bed, not caring that it was highly improper.

Empty.

He swung around, sweat pricking his brow. "Where is she?"

"What do you mean?" Peggy fisted a hand against her hip. "She was in here with you, then we come up here, and she gone. Seems like to me you'd be the one who know where she went."

Caleb felt across the rumpled blankets. Still warm.

He rocked back on his heels, speaking more to himself than the women. "She asked me to leave. She shut the door, and I sat on my cot. She never opened the door. She can't be gone."

His own breathing filled his ears. How was this even possible? Without a trace, without warning, and without his consent, Lena Lowrey had disappeared.

Chapter Thirteen

Pain. It pulsed in her skull, pushing behind her eyes and throbbing in her temples. Lena groaned. Had the absence of the persistent pain these past days made it that much more intolerable upon its return?

She couldn't believe she'd gotten so used to feeling normal again that she'd forgotten how much this hurt. Wait. Something wasn't right.

Lena bolted upright, and the pain intensified. She held her head, groaning and trying not to vomit. Finally, the dizziness subsided. She blinked in the dim light. The house sat shrouded in quiet shadows. She must have fallen asleep even though she'd been sure she'd be up all night, what with all the emotions crowding her heart. She breathed slowly. Not even the usual frogs and cicadas broke the stillness.

At least everyone else had gone back to sleep. She swung her legs off the side of the bed, only to find them hit the floor in the sitting area in the upper hallway.

She rose slowly, giving her body time to adjust, fighting against a surging worry. She had gone to bed in her room. The room Annabelle Ross had given her. Lena glanced around in the gloom. No cots. No snoring soldiers.

No Caleb.

Her throat constricted. That must mean...

"Momma!"

Lena lurched toward the bedroom door, but no sooner had she begun her stumbling steps than her mother burst from the room across the hall, the one that belonged to Annabelle Ross. Relief, so pungent it made her knees tremble, surged through her.

"Lena? Oh, honey!" Momma grabbed Lena's arm, steadying her. "What's happened?"

"You're...you're still here." A sob escaped her throat, and she sagged against Momma's shoulder. "Why are you still here?"

"Come now, baby, what are you talking about? I went to bed, remember?"

Lena lifted her head. "That was days ago."

Momma brushed damp hair from Lena's forehead. "You must have been dreaming. You probably fell asleep looking at those books."

"No, I..." She shook her head. "I've been gone for a long time."

Pushing a button on her old-school watch, Momma lit the digital face. "I went to bed an hour ago."

"So, wait. It's still the first day?"

Momma brushed a hand down Lena's back. "Why don't you come to bed?"

"No, I have to tell you what happened." Despite the pain clamoring for her attention, she had to get the story out while she had the chance. She had to let Momma know. "I put on a dress I found in the closet. It took me back in time to the Civil War."

In the small glow of the hall nightlight, Lena could see the concern on Momma's face.

"You have to believe me." The words tumbled free, desperate to find purchase. Someone had to believe her! "I know it doesn't make any sense. I know that. But it's true. It wasn't a dream."

Momma was quiet for a moment, then took Lena's hand and squeezed it. "You know the tumor...it does things to you."

"When I was there, I didn't hurt."

Momma drew her lip through her teeth, concern turning to deeper worry in her eyes.

"I was working as a nurse. Helping the soldiers. Teaching them about proper sanitation and better treatments. I think...yes, I think the tumor was gone. I had energy, and I felt good." She gathered strength, praying Momma would see. "Even though I had to use a makeshift toilet outside and you don't even want to know what brushing my teeth was like and...."

Tears glistened down Momma's tired cheeks. "How about we go to bed now?"

"I don't want to upset you, Momma, but it's true. I felt like I belonged there. I had a purpose." She allowed Momma to guide her to the bedroom. "And I met a man." Her heart wrenched at the thought of Caleb, of how they'd left things.

Momma hesitated, then hardened her words like she'd done when Lena was little and didn't want to obey. "Lena, you've had a very vivid dream. I'm happy to talk to you about it and hear all about what you dreamed the past would look like. But we have to admit it was a dream." Momma's voice hitched. "Otherwise it means the tumor—"

Lena stopped, snagging her mother to a halt alongside her. "It wasn't a dream."

Momma's voice trembled. "We were supposed to have our weekend, remember?"

Of course she remembered. She remembered everything. Why did Momma keep asking her if she remembered things? "I need you to believe me. It was almost as if God gave me a miracle. A strange, ridiculous, impossible miracle. But when I was there, I was healed. I could feel it. Now that I'm back here…"

"Stop it."

"But—"

"No." Momma pulled her arm again. "You had a dream. You're going to have the surgery. You're going to be just fine."

"I'm not, Momma."

Momma released her hand, and a sob bubbled out of her throat. "Please, stop this and let's go to bed."

Lena grabbed her mother in a tight embrace. "I love you, Momma. So much. You have always been there for me. But I'm dying…and you know it's true."

Momma stifled a sob. "It isn't fair!"

Lena pulled her close. "I know. Maybe it doesn't seem that way. But none of us knows how long our time will be. Who are we to say that it's not fair?"

She held tight while Momma's shoulders shook. "I

can't…I can't stand for you to leave me."

Lena fought back her own tears.

Momma's voice warbled. "I don't want to lose you. I've prayed and prayed God would grant a miracle and there would be another way."

"Maybe he did. I think he let me visit the past. Maybe it was so I could learn that even when I have no control over anything at all, he controls *everything*. Even things we think are completely impossible."

"That doesn't make any sense."

Maybe not, but she believed it. "Let me show you something." Lena pulled Momma toward the door that led to the balcony. To where she had shared her first kiss with Caleb days—or was it years?—ago. "I tested it. I want you to reach down in that little crack there. While I was in the past, I found a way to leave some clues for you. I didn't know how I would tell you about them, but that doesn't matter now. I'm here, and I've been given the chance to prove it to you."

Momma stared at her.

"Please. Just reach down into that crack and find the paper. If it's not there, then I'll know it was only a dream, and we'll never speak of it again. We'll continue our weekend, and I'll have the surgery."

Momma sniffled and wiped her eyes.

"But if it is there, will you promise we can at least discuss it?"

"Oh, Lena. What game is this? Did you write a note and hide it while I was asleep?"

"Just look. Please."

Finally, after what seemed an eternity of Momma

studying her, she knelt at the place Lena indicated. It was only the first part of what Lena had conjured. She had an entire plan. And if this was her opportunity to share it, then she would not miss it.

Momma slipped a piece of paper free. It was still there! Lena breathed a sigh of relief. She hadn't doubted…well, perhaps she had. But it was good to see the aged and crumbling piece of paper, now more than a century and a half old.

"It says, 'Proof that Lena was here. September 10, 1864. I love you, Momma.'" Momma looked up, her eyes glistening. "I love you, too." She rose. "But this only proves you wrote on an old scrap of paper."

Lena clasped her hands. "I knew you'd say that. So I thought of something else. I asked Caleb—you remember that man I told you about?—to cut a specific tree for me when he started chopping logs for Peggy's kitchen fire."

Momma started to look exasperated, and then more upset with every word Lena spoke.

"Oh, don't worry." Lena tried for a bit of humor to lighten the mood. "Annabelle was a little annoyed at first, but it passed quickly."

"Lena, this is ridiculous."

"Is it? Tell me. Where did you park the car when we got home from the restaurant?"

She crossed her arms. "Out under that giant oak. Why?"

"Would you believe me if we went down there right now and the tree was gone?"

"That's impossible."

Lena held out her hand. "Then let's go look, shall we? In eighteen sixty-four, that tree was nothing but a sapling."

"After we look, will you go to bed?"

"I promise."

Reluctantly, Momma followed her down the stairs and into the dark foyer, lit by the soft glow of another small nightlight. How different it seemed without her patients. She pushed the thought aside, moving carefully as the increasing pain in her head made it difficult to concentrate. But she must hide it. At least until she could prove herself.

Hopefully, Mr. Hylander hadn't set an alarm. Lena turned the knob and cracked the front door, and when no sirens sounded, opened it wide. Momma stepped to the door and without hesitation flipped the light switch.

The front porch flooded with cool light, chasing away shadows. Lena blinked in the harsh glare, pain nearly stealing her breath. Had she so soon forgotten the blue-white glow of artificial light?

Momma gasped. "Now, how in the world...?"

Lena stepped out onto the porch. The car was parked in exactly the same position, but the sweeping branches of the ancient oak were nowhere to be seen.

"See?" Lena used the side of the house for support. "I told you it was true."

Momma's mouth fell agape. A noise drew Lena's attention, and she looked back through the open doorway to see Mr. Hylander coming their way.

"Are you ladies all right?"

Lena shrugged, even though the pain behind her

eyes was pounding. "Sure. Momma just wanted to look at the tree."

The man frowned, his eyebrows tugging together. "Pardon?"

Lena gestured toward Momma, trying to keep her words steady. "Better ask her."

He looked at Lena for a moment but then stepped out onto the porch. "Something wrong, ma'am?"

"What?" Momma turned to look at him. "No, I was just, uh…" She glanced at Lena. "What happened to the tree?"

"What tree?"

"The big old oak that was right there by the house. I parked my car under it when we came back from the restaurant this evening."

Mr. Hylander turned his palms out. "I'm sorry, but there has never been a tree there. You must be mistaking it with the one in the backyard. That one's been there since the Civil War."

Interesting. They'd never cut the one Caleb was originally instructed to chop. How many other things would change if she lived in the past? Or, instead, had her presence always been intended for that time, and, therefore, would that make things the way they were supposed to be?

Oh, her head hurt too much for such musings. She'd made her point. Now it was time to get some rest.

"Oh, no, I am not mistaken," Momma insisted, her voice becoming shrill. "There was a giant tree"—she thrust her finger in that direction—"right *there*."

Mr. Hylander cleared his throat. "Ma'am, I have

been at this house for years, and my parents were here long before me. I assure you, you are mistaken. There has never been a tree there." He extended his arm toward the doorway. "Now, if you don't mind, perhaps it is best we get some rest?"

Lena closed her eyes. Yes. Rest would be good. She was starting to feel woozy. She closed her eyes against the black edges of her vision, finding it took entirely too much energy to draw a full breath. Would she be able to make it back up the stairs?

"Lena?"

She tried to answer, but though her lips moved, nothing came out. Why wouldn't her words work? Her tongue felt too thick for her mouth. She started to lean too far away from the house.

"Lena!"

Her mother's screech was the last thing she heard before everything went black.

"What you mean she disappeared?" Peggy pointed a long finger at him, as though that would make him spout a more logical answer.

Caleb picked up the yellow gown from the floor and rubbed it between his fingers. What had she said about the yellow dress? "She shut the door, and that was the last I saw of her. She never left the room."

Miss Ross shook her head. "That's not possible." They stood there a moment in silence, and then Miss

Ross brightened. "No one saw her come in, either. She must be adept at hiding. Perhaps she was quiet and you simply didn't see her exit."

"Hard to miss when I stared at the door the entire time."

Private Jenkins mumbled something from his cot in the hall, but Caleb ignored him. Peggy, however, lacked the decorum.

"Why was you staring at her door?"

Miss Ross's eyes widened. "Peggy! Don't ask such things."

Peggy eyed Caleb for a moment before grumbling her consent.

"Well," Miss Ross stated, attempting to cover Caleb's embarrassment and her maid's gaffe. "She can't have gone down from the windows, so she must have slipped out somehow."

As the women contemplated the possibilities, Caleb studied the gown in his hand. Why leave it behind? Assuming she'd left, which she hadn't—of that he was certain. That left only two possibilities. She'd jumped from the window and ran in the dark, or she'd slipped back to her own time.

He was uncomfortable with both theories, and could not stand idly by. He dropped the gown. "I'm going to look for her."

The two women stopped their chattering. Peggy gave him a sour face, but Miss Ross nodded. "Take some of the hardy men with you, if they're willing. We can't let her wander around in the dark."

Caleb strode from the chamber, only to find Private Jenkins already waiting with his boots on and a lantern in hand. Caleb paused, then clapped the man on the shoulder. Together, they descended the stairs and went out into the night.

How had he let this happen? He'd only thought to protect her from herself and from the men. It was the only way he could fathom to keep her safe in his absence. But in all of that, he'd neglected to tell her he wanted her to wait for him. If the war ended soon, like she seemed so sure it would, then he wanted to come back for her.

Court her.

Marry her.

But he'd told her none of those things. He'd thought he had more time, or at least a better time for announcing his intentions than the tense moments following Sergeant Wells's disgrace. The thought of the man had him grinding his teeth. He and Jenkins traipsed through the yard, Jenkins holding the lantern high, though no amount of light could chase the shadows from his thoughts.

"Where do you think she would have gone, Sergeant?"

The future. "I don't know."

"Odd how she just disappeared like that. I didn't hear her come out, either."

Caleb called her name. His voice carried on the still night air, but only cicadas answered. To his credit, Jenkins remained quiet for the rest of the trek, and by the time the sun began to tinge the sky orange, they had made three consecutively larger circles around the house. He'd seen the old slave quarters, the brick-making huts, and all manner of wildlife, but not a hint of a mysterious woman with quick wit and tempting curls.

She was gone.

Wherever she had come from, she had returned and left his life as easily as she had set upon it. His footsteps grew heavier with each trod back toward the house.

"I'm sorry for it, Sergeant." Compassion laced Jenkins's voice, and Caleb was glad for the company.

He stopped and turned to the shorter man. "Forgive me for not thanking you earlier. You didn't have to spend the night stomping through the woods."

Jenkins blew out the lantern and let it drop down to his side. "Know what it's like, loving a girl that's suddenly gone." He cleared his throat and looked past Caleb's shoulder. "Fever took mine. I was hoping we could find yours."

His. Lena Lowrey wasn't his. But heaven help him, he wanted her to be. How…and when…had that happened? He gave Jenkins a nod, and they resumed their trek to the porch. Had it happened the first time she looked upon him with only calm assessment and not the first hint of disgust? Or had it been when she stubbornly insisted on treating him and not allowing him to wallow in the loss of his eye? Perhaps it had been her quiet encouragement to get back to feeling useful without ever being condescending.

All of those things had deepened his feelings for her. He'd hoped such stirrings would fall flat and his attraction to a woman who was too bold, too strange, and too independent would be doused. Instead, her every move had done nothing but further fan the flame. He'd done everything in his power to keep from yearning for her. Had tried, and failed.

The yellow hospital flag hung limp in the early morning air, dangling from Rosswood's balcony and looking as listless as he felt. The crunch of their boots in the parched grass seemed only to echo the dryness he felt inside. How could he return to the life he had lived before Lena Lowrey?

He glanced to the heavens. *Maker of time, the span between us means nothing to you. Would you bring her back to me?*

So help him, if he ever saw her again, nothing on this earth would keep him from sweeping her into his arms and declaring his heart.

Chapter Fourteen

Maybe if she kept her eyes closed, she could hold on to the dream. But try as she might, it slipped through her fingers just as easily as she had slipped back from the past. The constant beeps of the monitor next to her grated on her frayed nerves. Slips of memory, the pleasure of a kiss, all faded under the garish noises.

She hated hospitals. Ironic, as she was supposed to have been a nurse. Momma snored softly, no doubt exhausted. The last time Lena awoke, it had been to find herself back in Jackson at River Oaks Hospital. She remembered nothing about Momma's account of her stop at the small local hospital or her helicopter ride to Jackson.

Lena slowly opened her eyes, the bluish light seeming gaudy. When had she fallen in love with the gentle glow of candlelight? Or the enjoyment of unhurried meals and a slower pace?

Probably the same time she had so quickly fallen in love with a man who would now be long dead. Tears welled and slid down her cheeks. How cruel that she should realize she loved him, now that he was lost to her forever. She could feel herself slipping and, somewhere deep within, knew she would not be long for this world.

Her throat burned, and she let the gentle tears course two trails of heartache down her cheeks. She must have completed whatever she needed to accomplish in eighteen sixty-four. Perhaps one of the soldiers she'd saved was needed to help end the war. Only, in a twist of heartless fate, she'd found her true love in a place she could never reach again. No amount of determination, money, or distance could return her to the past.

Oh, but why send her to the past to torment her heart, only to bring her back here to die? Why not leave her there? As soon as she'd come back, something had changed. She'd felt it. Her body was weaker, and even with the high doses of pain medications, her head felt tender and swollen. It almost seemed that while she'd been suspended in time, her tumor had grown quickly even though not much present time had elapsed. Time. Oh, what a fickle thing. It no longer made any sense to her.

With great effort, Lena turned her head to look at Momma. Would she be okay without her? It had been the two of them since Lena was a baby. Lena closed her eyes again and prayed that Momma would find happiness and a full life.

Let her find love. Let her do all the things she always dreamed of. She sacrificed so much for me. Please, Lord, let her find ease from stress and worry. Send her someone to bring her love, joy, and companionship. Do not leave her alone.

Peace filled her, and she slowly drew a breath. She'd wanted to feel love for a good man before she died, and she'd been given that chance. Maybe it wasn't meant to be anything more than that. God had known her longing and had granted her wish. It didn't even matter if it was real or not. It felt real to her. And that was enough. In the past, she'd had a fleeting chance to do the things she'd wanted out of life before it was too late. To be a nurse. To be needed. To love a man and sense his love in return.

If only she'd told Caleb how she truly felt. If she'd been brave enough to see that his anger stemmed from his care for her, then maybe she would have revealed her heart. Life was too short to hide under the fear of rejection. Wouldn't rejection have been better than this? This regret of never having told him she loved him?

She would never get the chance now. But maybe he already knew. She prayed he would know, and that he didn't think she left him by choice in her anger. Her pulse beat in her head, and her breaths felt harder to draw.

"Momma?" Her voice was scratchy and didn't even sound like her own. She reached a pale hand out through the rails, shocked at how weak she'd become. Had it not been only yesterday—or maybe the day before?—that she'd been standing with Momma on the porch at Rosswood? How had she grown so weak that fast?

"Lena? Oh, you're awake!" Momma slid from the patterned chair and onto the floor by the bed. She grasped Lena's hand, and tears pooled in her eyes.

"How long…have I been…asleep?" Why were her words so hard to form? She felt as though she were trying to speak with a mouth full of cotton.

"A long time, baby girl. Nearly three days, except for a few moments here and there." She tried to smile, but it faltered. "You're awake now, though. That's a good sign."

Lena struggled to bring air into her lungs, but tried not to let the effort show. It seemed her body was forgetting how to function. She might not have much time.

"I need you to listen."

"Hush, darling. You don't have to talk now. Just rest."

"No." She weakly squeezed Momma's hand. "I don't have…much time."

Momma's mouth quivered even as she shook her head. "But you do. Your surgery is going to happen. You'll be fine. You'll see."

Lena concentrated on another long breath, and Momma had to lean over the bed to catch her breathy words. "Just listen. I want you to go back to Rosswood after I'm gone."

Momma squeaked, but Lena squeezed her hand again. She didn't have much time now. She could feel herself slipping away.

"I'm going to get the doctor!"

"Please. Stay!" The force of the word took too much out of her, and she had to struggle for another breath.

Momma began to sob and pushed the nurse button. "Come quick!"

The intercom buzzed. Soon there would be a flurry of people.

"Momma." She dug deep for strength. *Please, give me the strength to say goodbye.* She sucked a gulp of air. "Promise me you'll go back. Maybe this is not the end. Maybe I'm meant to live the rest of my life in a different time."

"Oh, Lena!" Momma leaned over, draping herself over the rail. "The doctor will be here soon."

"Promise me you'll go. If I make it back, I'll leave something for you." Her eyesight blurred. First in tattered edges, and then Momma's face faded to gray before it disappeared. Lena closed her eyes. "Promise…please…"

"I promise." Momma shook her. "Please, Lena. Hold on!"

Beyond Momma's voice she heard another sound. The familiar laughter of men playing cards. The chirp of birds. And something more, beckoning her…

"Code blue!"

A jumble of voices filled the room, crushing out the other sounds. Caleb's voice. Calling for her….

She strained toward it. If only she could find one more breath…

"Lena!"

"Love…you…Momma."

The constant beep at her ear slowed…then turned to a long, shrill tone. Her body surrendered, and the pain flowed away from her. Warm light swelled, and something beautiful entertained her senses, drawing her toward overwhelming peace. Her soul reached for the One she had known for years, yet desperately longed to see. The light erupted into a million colors, and then she drifted into a serene sleep.

Something was wrong. Caleb jerked from his pallet, startling his tent mate as he jumped to his feet, tripping over scattered ammunitions, rucksacks, and canteens.

Lena.

He could have sworn he heard her calling to him. He fumbled with the tightened tent strings, his fingers seeming too thick to function. They finally succumbed to his efforts, and he thrust back the canvas. The late October mornings had finally begun to cool, hinting winter might not be too long in coming. He scanned the trees, still green despite the cooling air, but saw nothing.

"What are you doin', Sarg?" Jenkins's sleepy voice followed him from the tent, not seeming alarmed.

"I heard her." Caleb stood outside the tent, his eyes scanning in every direction.

If she could appear at Rosswood, then surely she could appear in an army camp. But only men in tattered and mismatched grays moved about in the early morning light, seeking to find watered-down coffee and scraps of hardtack around campfires before they started daily drills.

Jenkins clapped him on the shoulder. "She's not

here, Caleb."

In the weeks since Lena had disappeared, he'd been glad for Paul Jenkins's steady company. He might not have been able to leave Rosswood and return to duty had it not been for the man's gentle words of irrefutable logic. She wasn't coming back. He'd stood guard over her door, had barely slept each night until he was forced to return to his unit. He had hoped she would step into the upper hall, radiant in her yellow gown, and all would be right with his world again. But she'd never appeared, and each day his world seemed a little darker for the lack of her.

Caleb had grown accustomed to the emptiness taking up residence in his chest, but today was different. He couldn't explain it, but he sensed somewhere deep within him that something had changed.

"I heard her, Paul. She was calling to me."

Jenkins gave his shoulder a squeeze, too kind to point out Caleb was going mad.

Men moved about camp, paying them no mind. They were half-starved, and many of them had long since started to question keeping up the fight. Caleb's duty was nearly complete, and he wouldn't sign up again. All he wanted was to find Lena, make her his own, and start a life free of the struggles of war. Their cause was surely lost, and ever since Lena had peppered him with questions about where slavery fit into his faith, Caleb had lost all desire to keep up the struggle. Now he simply prayed he wouldn't have to face another battle.

"You were just dreaming," Jenkins said softly, trying to draw Caleb's desperate gaze from the fringes of the bustling camp. "You know she isn't here."

She wasn't here. She wasn't at Rosswood. So, where was she? He'd searched three more times before he, Jenkins, and three others were brought back to duty. Every movement, every flash of color he caught from the corner of his eye had him searching for yellow ruffles, but she had slipped from him like smoke through his fingers.

The wind stirred, and on it, he heard it again. "There! Listen."

Jenkins sighed but turned his ear in the direction Caleb pointed. But the clamor of the men making ready for the day's drills made it impossible to hear.

"Men! Quiet!" His voice boomed out over those in his squad, but instead of halting their movements, they all scrambled for weapons to point in the direction Caleb faced.

Jenkins mumbled something under his breath.

Finally, everyone settled, the soldiers looking for the enemy with weapons at the ready as Caleb merely listened for the voice he longed to hear. He heard nothing other than the rustle of leaves and the call of birds. But he could not deny the unsettling sense that something had happened. She was out there...somewhere. He could feel it.

Caleb looked at Jenkins, but his face remained as concerned as everyone else's.

Before he gave himself enough time to contemplate it, Caleb dismissed his men and turned back to the tent to find his boots. "I have to go."

Jenkins grabbed his arm. "What? What are you

talking about? We have drills. You can't go anywhere."

"I don't care." Caleb extracted his arm and surged back into the tent. "I have to go back to Rosswood."

Jenkins followed. "Are you mad? They'll charge you with deserting!"

"So be it." Caleb snatched his kepi down over his disheveled hair. "Whatever punishment they give will be worth it."

Moments later, he saddled a horse without permission and was galloping toward his only hope for the future.

Chapter Fifteen

Warm sunlight washed across her face, and Lena breathed deeply through clear lungs. Birds twittered, begging her to open her eyes. But she couldn't. Not yet. For another moment she had to hang on to this lingering sense she'd had—this nearness to the Lord's goodness that for a moment she had almost been able to touch.

Suddenly the shroud of otherworldliness around her shattered, and her eyes flew wide. Had she died? She blinked. A canopy bed, wrapped in mosquito netting...

She bolted upright, a wave of relief that she felt no pain weakening her knees. Lena held on to the bedpost and sank her bare toes into the woven rug. She let her gaze drift from the wood floor up to the high ceilings.

She'd returned to Rosswood. But how? The gown had not come back with her that night. And then she'd been at the hospital...

None of that mattered. She was here, and she wouldn't waste another moment without seeing Caleb. If she'd been granted a chance to say goodbye, she would not miss it. She hurried to the door, pausing just as her hand grasped the knob.

Glancing down at her attire, she was glad she'd paused. Still dressed in a revealing hospital gown! Lena rolled her eyes. She'd never explain that one. Whirling around, she headed for the wardrobe and flung it open. Would there be anything in there?

The yellow gown, bright as it had ever been, awaited her. Next to it, Lena found a neatly folded chemise, bloomers, and other bygone necessities. She quickly pulled them on, tugging the laces of a corset she was surprised she didn't mind wearing. Now where were...ah, there. Lena plucked two stockings from the back corner and pulled them on, having to tuck them beneath the bloomers. She should probably have put them on first. She had to hurry. After finding a pair of soft slippers, Lena pulled them on, marveling at the perfect fit.

A petticoat came next, tied around the corset. She reached for the gown, then paused. She wanted to look her best, didn't she? Taking up most of the other side of the wardrobe was a whale-boned hoop skirt. Smiling, she settled it over the first petticoat and tied the strings, then slipped on another petticoat, this one meant to hide the hoop's ribbing.

She gently removed the yellow gown, praying putting it on would not suddenly take her back to the hospital room. She closed the wardrobe, her gaze snagging on the mirrored doors. Her eyes looked bright with no dark bags underneath them and no taint of pain.

Her heart galloped. What if her time in the present

had ended but the Lord really had granted the rest of her life in the past?

No. She must not get her hopes up. Not yet. She might very well still be in a hospital room, granted only a quick reprieve.

She studied herself in the mirror, letting her gaze drift to the rest of her face. How in the world...? She reached up to touch her chocolate curls, which had been piled and artfully arranged on the top of her head, leaving only a few free to frame her face.

Lena closed her eyes and drew a breath. A dream only, then. A chance to speak to Caleb as a lady and then be gone from this world entirely. Strangely, that idea did not scare her as it once had. Not after she'd felt the intangible...*something* that had enveloped her before she awoke here. If all of eternity felt like that fleeting moment, then she would surely welcome it.

But please, be with Momma. Send her someone, that she might not be alone until I can see her again when we both stand in your presence.

Balancing her excitement with trepidation, she rubbed the fabric of the yellow gown. One last time to wear it. One last moment in the past.

Carefully pulling it over her head, lest she disturb her hair, Lena finally got it settled properly and buttoned. Holding her breath, she waited, but did not disappear back to the present. She released the air from her lungs, marveling that she could do so freely and without pain.

Smoothing the soft fabric, she lingered in front of the mirror. If she didn't know any better, she would think she belonged here. She felt like Cinderella about to go to the ball. Well, if Cinderella had been dropped into a war and her prince was a soldier with an eye patch. Drawing back her shoulders, Lena crossed the room and opened the door, only to find the hallway empty.

Her stomach knotted. Had she returned to Rosswood...but in the wrong time? Was she in the present after all, but had not noticed the shift? Mouth feeling full of sand, she studied the furnishings but could not remember from which time she had seen them. Mr. Hylander had done so well keeping period furniture in the house, it was nearly impossible to tell.

Only one thing left to do, then. She must go downstairs. Gathering her gown, she slowly descended the stairs, then turned to face the front door.

It was too quiet. She released the dress, letting it sweep the top of the floor. With the hoops underneath, she wasn't tripping over the length. Finally, just as she thought her heart would gallop out of her chest, she heard a voice.

"That only leaves seven, and we can keep them all down here. Lawd, it be good to get..."

Lena turned just as Peggy exited the parlor.

Caleb pushed the poor beast to its limits. The horse's hooves churned up damp earth and sent him thundering across abandoned fields. He leapt a crumbling fence and was nearly unseated when the mare stumbled. It took less than an hour at a reckless gallop to reach Rosswood, but it seemed an eternity.

His heart pounded nearly as fast as the horse's stride as he made the turn to the house. The mansion stood proud in the early morning mist, the yellow hospital flag the only blemish on its fair complexion.

Caleb lowered his head and leaned deep into the horse's rhythm, praying he would find what he longed for at the end of the road that split the fallow lands surrounding the house. He jerked the horse to a stop, and it nearly reared. Righting himself, Caleb leapt from the saddle as the creature snorted and pawed at the ground.

In his haste, he nearly forgot to scoop the reins and tie them to the post, but he would be in more hot water for losing a horse than he would be for leaving camp without permission. Fingers scraping the dewed grass, he knotted the reins but left the mare room to graze the damp stalks. The horse would need water soon.

But first he had to know.

The front door cracked open before he could reach it, and Peggy's face scowled at him. "What's happened?"

Caleb paused, the foolishness of his actions finally catching up with him. He drew himself up tall. "Nothing has happened. All is well."

Peggy stared at him, her face nearly wedged between door and frame.

"Is...uh...all well here?"

She lifted a dark eyebrow. "Why you ask?"

He tapped his toe. "Just tell me. Is she here?"

"Miss Belle don't ever leave this here house,

so 'course she here."

The muscle in his jaw ticked. This was utter madness. He had let himself lose his wits pining for Lena and had conjured a more favorable explanation than the one that often haunted him. What if she really had fallen through the window and someone had taken her before he could find her?

Caleb clenched his fists and turned back toward the heaving horse.

"But if you mean the other lady, well…."

He whirled around as Peggy pulled the door wide and stepped back. He strained forward, his heart seeming to reach out even as his feet remained rooted. Movement parted the shadowed interior. A flash of dandelion.

There, in radiant yellow, like a sun breaking through the dark clouds, stood his Amberlena Lowrey.

He'd come. How had he known? She fought back tears. It didn't matter. She'd been granted this moment. This one precious moment to drink in his features, to savor the thrill that lit his eye and to know, if only for this instant, that the one she loved wanted to see her.

Lena couldn't move. Could hardly breathe. How could she say goodbye? What words would do justice to all she felt and all she would never know? Transfixed in the doorway, she hardly noticed Peggy's laugh or Caleb's pounding boots across the porch as he reached out for her.

She slipped her hand into his rough palm, her pulse thudding in her ears. He gently pulled her onto the porch, and she vaguely recognized the door closing behind her. Caleb held fast to her hand, an anchor in the storm of emotions that pounded her senses.

"You came back."

His voice held such relief, such joy, that the tears she'd tried to contain slipped down her cheeks. "I'm sorry I yelled at you to leave me alone." She pressed her lips together. "If I could have my way, I would never leave you again."

Caleb squeezed her fingers and drew her closer, the scent of horse and earth reminding her how masculine this fierce man before her truly was.

"Then stay. Stay here with me, Lena." He reached up and took one of her curls, gently twisting it around his finger.

"I don't think I have a choice. But I am thankful to have gotten the chance to say goodbye."

He dropped the curl, his brow furrowing. "Good-bye?"

How could she explain? He would never understand.

"I know our time is not what you're used to," Caleb said, his entreating voice tearing at her raw heart. "I'm sure you have more comforts and pleasures awaiting you at home than could ever be found here." He stepped closer, placing his hands on her shoulders. "I have naught to offer but starved lands, a losing army, and the boundless devotion of a maimed soldier." His hand, warm on her cheek, could not rival the heat in his words. "But I pray beyond all reason that it will be enough."

Her mouth opened, but no words escaped.

Caleb gently took her chin and tilted her head back. "Forgive me for doubting you. You have been nothing but sincere and honest. I believe whatever you say is truth, because I value you and your word above all others, save the Creator himself."

"You…believe me?"

"As mad as it might make us both, I do. Who am I to say what miracles exist or limit their power?"

"I…" Her voice hitched, and he released her chin to smooth away the emotion escaping her eyes. "If only I could stay." She gathered her resolve, steeling her heart. She must say these things while she could. Taking his hand in hers, she peered up at him. "Sergeant Caleb Dockery, I would leave everything I have ever known for just another moment in your arms. Simply knowing you has erased the ache I always tried to bury."

He smiled, but she squeezed his fingers before he could speak.

"But I fear I have been granted only a short time, and I must use it wisely." She straightened her shoulders and looked at him, allowing all that she felt to shine through her eyes. "I love you."

His grin, broad as the sweeping sky, nearly stopped her heart. Caleb pulled her into his embrace, his strong arms enveloping her in a longing that threatened to sweep her away. Without hesitation, he lowered his lips to hers, and the sensation weakened her knees.

This moment, this one blissful moment, would be the perfect ending to her story. She tangled her fingers in the hair at the base of his neck and surrendered to every feeling she had tried to suppress.

Love. Joy. Desire. Longing. They all swept through her as she pushed herself deeper into his embrace, trying to hold on to every sweet movement of his lips.

Too soon, he lifted his head. "My sweet Lena. My love for you cannot be bound by time or distance, and it knows no end, even until eternity."

She reached for him again. Let her days end here, with the declaration of his love upon his lips and her own tasting the everlasting sweetness of them.

Merriment danced in his eye, and he kept his mouth just above her reach. "Not another until you give me one final answer."

If only she could.

"Marry me, Amberlena Lowrey. Walk by my side through the trials of life. Be my helpmate, my confidant, and someday, the mother of my children."

Joy erupted through her. "Nothing would make me happier."

He leaned down again, but this time it was she who turned away. "But I do not know how long I will be able to stay here. I fear my time is limited."

He pulled her tight against him, and she rested her head in the soothing place between his neck and shoulder. "Well, then, it seems we have something in common. For which of us knows how many days we will be granted upon this earth? Who among us knows the measure of our days?"

"Truer words have not been spoken, my love."

Caleb drew her back to look at her again. "Then let us live each moment to the fullest and savor all that we have. Agreed?"

"Agreed."

He looped her hand over the crook of his arm and, ever the gentleman, led her down the steps of the house. "Now, my darling betrothed, walk with me for a time and let us make our plans for the future before I must face the consequences of leaving my unit."

Her heart full, Lena leaned into his side and let him guide her. She had never truly known how many days she had. The diagnosis had told her when to expect her death, but even the doctors could never know how many days God granted, or *when* he granted them, for that matter. But whatever he blessed her with, they would be enough. And for as many days as she was granted, she would love with abandon and cherish every moment.

For what did time truly matter? It was but a measurement that fell short, not a constraint that could bind her. She would make the most of whatever time God granted. "Have I told you I love you?"

Caleb chuckled. "Tell me every moment, and I shall tell you the same. For never shall I grow weary of knowing it."

Lena rested her head on his shoulder as they walked, and something within her stirred. Pausing, she turned to look back up at the house, shielding her eyes from the sun. A figure stood on the balcony, looking below. Annabelle?

Before she could say anything, and despite standing out in the open, Caleb drew her into his arms again. Not even time itself could contain her joy.

Epilogue

Celia Ann pulled the damp March air into lungs that still felt too raw from sorrow, hoping it would calm the pounding in her chest. Carl wrapped his arm around her shoulders and let her linger on the porch steps for as long as she needed.

She peered up at him beneath Rosswood's massive white columns, grateful for his strength. His blue eyes held tenderness behind his wire-rimmed glasses and spoke a depth of emotion that had truly been an answer to Lena's request. Carl loved her, of that she was certain. And oh, how she needed all he could give today.

"We can always turn back," he said, giving her a squeeze.

She shook her head. "No. I need to see it."

Carl released her shoulders to lift their bags, and memories came rushing back to her. Had it truly been only five months since she had stood on this very porch with Lena, shocked to see the giant tree missing? Had it been so short a time since they had made all their plans for the future, plans that would never come to pass?

Fighting back tears, she waited as Carl tapped on the door. Mr. Hylander opened it, his friendly smile compassionate.

"Miss Lowrey, thank you for coming." He shook hands with Carl and gestured for them to enter.

Celia made it only two steps past the threshold. The men discussed the arrangement of the two rooms Carl had booked for them for the night, but she didn't know if she could stay. How could she stand this twisting in her gut even to fulfill Lena's request she return?

Carl's steady strength and gentle love had helped her survive these past months without Lena, but she didn't think she was strong enough to bear the assault of memories this house brought. Not yet. If it hadn't been for Mr. Hylander's call and insistence, she might have never returned.

Hands trembling, she spoke up. "Forgive me. I don't know if I can stand to be here long." Gaining Mr. Hylander's eyes, she tried to keep her voice steady. "Please, what did you have to show me that you could not tell me on the phone?" Tears scalded her eyes. "And what does it have to do with my daughter?"

Mr. Hylander motioned toward the library. "Yes, of course. Let's get right to it." They stepped into the room. "The shelving in here was beginning to sag, and as we were doing the remodeling and repairs, we found something exceedingly peculiar when we removed them."

"Oh?" Carl guided Celia deeper into the room where Lena had sat and looked over the plantation diary, trying to take an interest because Celia enjoyed the history.

"Behind the shelving we discovered a strange section of the woodwork. It came free, revealing a small cubby inside."

Carl leaned closer, the historian in him clearly intrigued. "A secret compartment! Did they hide valuables in there during the war?"

Mr. Hylander gave a wry smile. "Valuable, yes. But not in the way you would think."

She rubbed her temples. At another time, this would have likely fascinated her, but right now she merely wished she had not been summoned here for something meaningless.

"As you can imagine," Mr. Hylander continued above the crinkle of something in his hands, "my family was rather unsure what to do with such an odd discovery, but we finally decided it would be best if we simply handed it over to you."

Celia finally looked at him, and he held out a bundle wrapped in parchment paper. "We found this hidden in the wall. Do you have any idea how it got there?"

She frowned. Had Mr. Hylander summoned her to accuse her of doing something in the house when they'd stayed before? Her mind raced back to the paper Lena had shoved in the upper balcony doorway. Had she...?

Celia took the package, and her heart seemed to stop. Written across the package in choppy script she read, *Please give this to my momma, Celia Ann Lowrey, when she returns like she promised she would. Lena.*

She looked up at Mr. Hylander. This couldn't be possible. How would Lena have been able to get something behind the bookshelves and into the wall?

The man spread his hands. "And now you can see our confusion over the matter, and why I wanted to wait to tell you in person. We have not opened it, since it's addressed to you, though I must admit, I am exceedingly curious."

Remembering all the strange things Lena had said, Celia's hands began to tremble. She lowered herself to the settee, pulling free a frayed cord holding the packaging together. Gently, she peeled back the wrapping, revealing a stack of folded and sealed papers underneath.

The one on the top read "open first" in Lena's sloppy script.

Celia turned it over, feeling the curious eyes of the men on her. It was sealed with a glob of wax, the initials LD embossed across it. She slipped her finger under the wax and the yellowed page released.

Pulse thudding, she opened the letter.

January 24, 1866

Dear Momma,

Thank you for coming back to Rosswood as you promised. If Mr. Hylander stayed true to his remodeling plans as he mentioned to us in our visit, then you should have found this letter not too long after I had to leave you. Lucky for me Annabelle returned from New York quite changed from the shy girl I taught to tend patients, and her sense of adventure allowed me to create a secret compartment in the wall before they put in new shelving.

I'm sorry I had to leave you, Momma. Know that I miss you and ever shall.

Celia put her fist to her mouth. This couldn't be true!

I know it sounds crazy, but all the things I told you that happened to me were true. I don't know why, and I did try to use the dress to visit you, but I couldn't. I think it may have been because I somehow kind of died there, so now I cannot get back. But I promise, I am very much alive.

Tears slipped out of her eyes, but Celia couldn't stop reading.

Remember the tree and the paper I showed you? This is all true, even though it doesn't make sense. But then, miracles seldom do. Please know that even though I had to leave you, I have found a wonderful life here. Some things I don't think I will ever get used to, mostly the lack of indoor plumbing and hot showers! Cherish those, especially in the winter!

I told you, there at the end, about the man I had met. Caleb mustered out of the army just before the Lincoln assassination, and we were wed soon after. Oh, how I wish you could have been here. You would have loved to see it!

Annabelle and I have become dear friends. You

wouldn't believe the adventures she has been on! Anyway, she promised I could come here every year, and every year we would add a letter to this hidden compartment in the wall. A compartment I pray no one finds until after our visit to Rosswood when Mr. Hylander remodels the library.

Trembling, she turned the paper over.

Be sure to live, Momma. None of us knows how much time we have. Don't hesitate to tell Carl how you feel about him, and promise me you will hold nothing back. See the world like you always wanted, and let yourself love to the fullest. I pray you find the happiness with him that I have found with Caleb.

I must go now, as Annabelle has company and Mr. Harper has hired a photographer. Taking a picture is much more complicated here than it would be at home, and I cannot miss it. It is my final surprise for you.

When we went to eat in Lorman, I told you about finding a picture of Rosswood on the wall at the restaurant. Go and see it. Caleb and I will be standing next to Peggy, Annabelle and Matthew, and their kin, Lydia and Charles Harper. Proof that all of this is true.

I wish you a lifetime of love and happiness, and I will love you through all of time.

Your daughter,
Lena

Sobbing now, Celia flipped through the stack of envelopes. They were not dated every year, and sometimes there was a several year gap between them, but the stack was thick. A treasure, to be sure! She caressed the final one, dated 1910.

"Well, darling, what is it?" Carl gripped her shoulder.

Celia pulled the letters to her chest, a profound sense of peace washing over her. Her baby had been given another chance at a full life, and had found love and contentment. She drew a deep breath and rose, thanking Mr. Hylander for giving the treasure to her.

"If you don't mind, I think I should take her up to her room to rest," Carl said, gently easing Celia to her feet.

Mr. Hylander, ever gracious, agreed, though she could see the curiosity written across his features.

Still stunned, she took the stairs to the top floor. While Carl set their bags on the wood floor and pulled out the keys to their rooms, Celia checked the slot in the wall where Lena had hidden her first sliver of proof but didn't find anything.

Nerves too aflame to stay still, Celia opened the balcony door and stepped outside, looking over the expanse of land. How much had it changed over the years? How many times had Lena stood on this very spot?

Movement drew her attention, and she looked down, her breath lodging in her throat. Below, a couple stepped arm in arm from the porch. The man, clad in a Confederate uniform, escorted a brunette woman in a wide yellow gown.

Celia rubbed her eyes. Hadn't she seen that girl in yellow the first time she'd been here? Yes. The girl, with dark hair like Lena's, had been running toward the iron gate and then had strangely disappeared…

She leaned further over the rail. The couple paused at the end of the walkway, and the woman turned to look up at her, shielding her eyes from the sun.

Lena!

The man turned her toward him, an eye patch covering one eye. Then he took her in his arms, and as he lowered his head for a kiss, they faded from sight.

Celia closed her eyes, whispering a prayer of thanks. She stood there a moment longer, then a sudden wild thought gripped her. And why not? Life was short and Lena was right. She needed to live it now, because she didn't know how much time she had. Whirling around, she rushed back inside, tears drying on her face.

"Carl!"

He dropped the keys and rushed to her, his brown hair flopping across his forehead. "What's wrong?"

"I saw them! The couple they said walks around Rosswood."

He looked dubious. "You did?"

She squeezed his hand. "It was Lena!"

Compassion filled his eyes. "Now, honey, you know that's not—"

"Oh, but it is *true*." She held up the letters. "And I can prove it. Come on, get our stuff. We have to go."

He gave a nod. "I wondered if this would be too hard on you."

"On the contrary." She wrapped an arm around his neck and planted a kiss firmly on his lips, savoring his surprise. "It was exactly what I needed."

Without waiting for his response, she hurried down the stairs, leaving Carl to gather their small bags and scramble after her.

"We thank you for your hospitality," she said, finding Mr. Hylander at the bottom of the stairs. "But I'm afraid Carl and I cannot stay."

Mr. Hylander offered a smile. "I understand. But perhaps sometime…if you wouldn't mind…"

"After I have had time to read all of the letters, I will share them with you."

"My family and I are most curious about it. Thank you!"

Celia entwined her fingers with Carl's. "Maybe we'll come back during our honeymoon, and I'll tell you all about it."

Carl's face split into a wide grin. "Does this mean you are finally accepting my proposal?"

"I am."

Mr. Hylander offered his congratulations, and after Carl returned the keys, they stepped out into a bright day.

Carl dropped the bags at the bottom of the steps and wrapped her in a hug. "I don't know what you read in there, but whatever it was, I am glad it made you this happy." He paused, searching her eyes. "But I don't want an answer based on fleeting emotion. Are you sure?"

She kissed him again, longer this time. When she

pulled back, she wondered why it had taken her so long. "Of course I do. You know I love you. I was just afraid to let myself hope in a future for us."

Carl grinned. "I'll take any future, so long as you're in it."

"So, let's not wait! I don't need a fancy wedding. A trip to the judge will do the job."

He pulled her close. "Anything you want."

She entwined their fingers, and they gathered their bags, the feeling of a fresh start a balm to her heart. Lena had lived. She had loved. And her beautiful daughter wanted her to do the same.

"Where to, love?" Carl asked, tossing their bags in the trunk of his Mercedes.

"To the nearest justice of the peace." She gave him a wink. "But first we have to stop at a restaurant in Lorman. I have something to show you."

Dear reader,

I hope you enjoyed Lena and Caleb's story. If you would take a few moments to leave a review online, I would truly appreciate it. And, if you haven't yet read The Accidental Spy Series, you'll get to meet up with Annabelle and Peggy again as they get caught up in the abduction attempt and assassination of Abraham Lincoln.

Thank you for taking this trip with me. Until we meet again!

Historical note

This novella muddies the line between fact and fiction, so I would like to let you know where (other than time travel, of course!) I changed the facts. Rosswood Plantation is a real place in Lorman, Mississippi, where you can visit for tours and stay at the bed-and-breakfast. It's currently run by Mr. Ray Hylander, a wonderful gentleman I've had the pleasure of getting to know over the time he's allowed me to keep using Rosswood in my books. If you stay at Rosswood, you'll enjoy a delectable breakfast prepared by Peggy, the lovely lady who I adored so much I borrowed her name for the character in my stories.

While visiting Lorman, be sure to stop at the Old Country Store. It does indeed have everything I mentioned in the story, from the wonderful Mr. D, to the antiques, to the "Best Fried Chicken in the World." It has been featured on the Food Network and the Travel Channel, and you will not want to miss it. The only thing you won't find is a portrait of my characters on the wall.

Mr. Hylander never found anything hidden behind the shelves in the library, and to my knowledge, there are no soldiers buried on the land. You can, however, see the diary and plantation records kept by Dr. Walter Ross Wade, the historical original owner of the house, along with his journal about his courtship and marriage to Mabella Chamberlain (who we believe owned the yellow gown). Guests also report seeing a Civil War era couple walking the lawn. While I never saw them during my own visit, it made for another interesting twist for the story.

To find out more about the history of the house and to make plans to visit, go to

www.RosswoodPlantation.net

Special Thanks

I'd like to thank Mr. Ray Hylander for allowing me to use not only Rosswood itself, but for being gracious enough to let me write him into my fanciful tale. I'd also like to thank his mother, Miss Jean Hylander, who first gave me permission to use the house, let me poke into every nook and cranny, and shared with me the fascinating history of Rosswood. Without you, I would have never had this crazy idea for a time traveling dress. Thank you for allowing me the privilege of taking pictures with it and for the opportunity to meet your wonderful family.

About the Author

 Stephenia H. McGee writes stories of faith, hope, and healing set in the Deep South. After earning a degree in Animal and Dairy Sciences, she discovered her heart truly lies with the art of story. She put pen to page and never looked back. Visit her at www.StepheniaMcGee.com for books and updates, and sign up for her newsletter for new releases, monthly giveaways and more.

Made in the USA
Monee, IL
11 October 2021